MW01109087

#1 HEROES OF DISTANT PLANETS SERIES

STRANGE LANDS

BY ANDERSON ATLAS

To: Daniel!
Have a great time in
my world!

ANDERSONATLAS

Synesthesiabooks.com
520-869-9649
thelostspells@gmail.com

This book is a work of fiction. Names, characters, places, and incidents either are products of the author's imagination or are used fictitiously. Any resemblance to actual events or locales or persons, living or dead, is entirely coincidental.

Copyright © 2016 Anderson Atlas and Synesthesia Books. All rights reserved.

Name: Atlas, Anderson
Title: Surviving the Improbable Quest
Description: Trade paperback edition 2: Synesthesia Books, 2016
Identifiers
ISBN-10: 0-9974788-7-X
ISBN-13: 978-0-9974788-7-7
Subjects: Paraplegic Hero Young Adult, alien world travel, Power of positive thought and bravery
BISAC: Juvenile Fiction / Science Fiction
Wholesale Available from IngramSparks

ACKNOWLEDGEMENTS:

Thank you to all that supported me through this novel including my family for putting up with my writing and drawing zeal. Thank you to my critique group members: Pam, Elaine, Kate, Marilyn, and Elise.

I also need to thank my editor whose expertise helped me conquer my blind spots! Thank you Brandi Wigginds for you hard work. I recommend her editing services any day of the week! Contact her at hildegartbookreviews@gmail.com

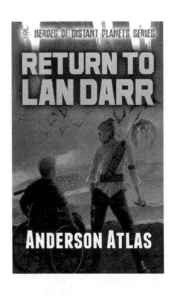

Book 2:

Return to Lan Darr

is a Must Read!
AndersonAtlas.com/ReturnToLanDarr

Book 3 of the Heroes of Distant Planets Series:

IMMORTAL SHADOW

go to AndersonAtlas.com/ImmortalShadow

"Oh, the THINKS you can think up if only you try!" -Dr. Seuss.

Dr. Seuss is my eternal inspiration for this story and maybe for every story and creature I've ever created.

STRANGE LANDS

BY ANDERSON ATLAS

Strange Lands

Contents:

Anderson Atlas

Strange Lands

By Anderson Atlas

Anderson Atlas

Chapter I
Born to Race

Allan Westerfield strolls down a long corridor toward the huge indoor pool, hearing roars from the crowd and echoes from the swim meet's announcer. His nerves are tight, twitching. He's used to being in front of crowds, wearing only a speedo; that's not his problem. This is the largest crowd he's ever raced in front of and the most important swim meet of his burgeoning swim career.

A man emerges from the shadow of a side doorway, startling Allan. It's his large bear-like principal, Mr. Greggory, wearing a dark blue shirt and a silver tie, the school colors. The man is an imposing figure: six foot something, black hair graying at the temples, and a stare that can freeze souls.

"Before you swim, Mr. Westerfield," Mr. Greggory begins, his voice deep like an Addams Family member. "I feel obligated to remind you of why you were let into our prestigious school in the first place. You're here to win. If you do not live up to your repute, you will eventually be expelled due to your poor grades and lackluster attitude."

"Uh–" Allan's tongue is tied, his entire body stiff as a board.

"I was informed yesterday that you failed your last math exam. You cannot swim with your grades." Mr. Greggory lets his scowl fall from his face and replaces it with a large, fake smile.

Another swimmer in a bright red one-piece passes, her towel over her shoulder, earbuds in her ears.

Mr. Greggory sighs and straightens his tie. "I'm a forgiving man, as you know. So I've decided not to tell the judges. All you must do is beat Southern Catholic High. We'll have to do something about that test score for your record to stand, but I'm willing to help so that our school reputation is not tarnished."

Allan swallows hard, his voice lost in his chest. He had no idea he'd failed his math test and that it dropped his GPA to an unacceptable level. He hated school, expressly Greenville Academy, especially the teachers, particularly the principal.

Mr. Greggory rests his large hand on Allan's shoulder, pressing down firmly. "If you do not win, I'll see that any future you think you have in this sport is thoroughly demolished. Do I make myself clear?"

Allan nods and is pushed down the corridor toward the pool.

The indoor pool is huge, with bleachers on either side of the swim lanes, the air sharp with the smell of chlorine. Allan's mother is sitting near the main entrance. The rest of the stands are full of classmates and strangers. Allan mills near his team, waiting until his name is called. Mac, his best friend, tries speak to him, but his brain can't focus on what he's saying. All he can do is concentrate on winning his race. If he fails, his life will go down in a ball of flame.

Allan's name is called, and he steps to the edge of the pool. His feet feel numb on the cold, wet tiles, and he can't wait to jump in the water. The announcer reads his stats, and finally, Allan is allowed onto the dive block. He waits as the other swimmers are introduced, breathing deep and ignoring the doubt that is always with him. He never expected to win this meet. His time wasn't even close to the dead-eyed Chris Tanker, the Southern Catholic's swim god, who was two lanes away, waving to the crowd, pumping his fist in the air.

The swimmers ready and the crowd goes silent.

The gun goes off. Allan jumps, his start flawlessly timed. He powers through the water like a harpoon, forgetting the ten other kids he is swimming next to. It's only him now, just how he likes it. The water is another world to Allan, a strange atmosphere, but freeing, the only place he feels at home and in control. When he swims, he imagines himself in a deep ocean full of other creatures or sunken cities. He usually pretends he's being chased by great white sharks or by enormous squid.

Not today. Today, Allan is focused on nothing but his technique. His head breaks into the air and he sucks in a breath. He kicks as hard as he can and reaches as far as his arms will go. *Move it! Faster!* he yells to himself.

The intense roar of the crowd deadens every time Allan's head falls below the waterline. But when his ears rise above the splashes he can hear them again. Someone yells his name, and then the sound vanishes, replaced by the silent peacefulness of being underwater. Allan feels his heart beat in his chest like a caged monster. Energy pumps through his body at dizzying speeds. His arms pull the water, and his legs power a tornado behind him.

Allan's eyes follow the dark blue tiles at the bottom of the pool until they end in a 'T.' At the perfect moment, he tucks his head under him and twists. Memory, deep in his muscles, guides his every move.

The boy in the next lane falls farther and farther behind. Allan's lead fuels the clamor of the crowd. The echo is almost deafening. He knew he was fast, but this is a state competition, and on paper his opponents are all faster than him. He gasps air and powers himself through the water.

Push it now! Allan strains every muscle, burns through every breath and lets himself become utterly silent inside.

Allan reaches up and touches the end of his lane, letting his body collide with the pool wall. His ears drain of water, and the roar of the crowd powers out the announcer's voice. Allan looks around. His mother is jumping up and down, so is Mac. Everyone's looking at him. Confused, Allan looks at the other swimmers. Most smile or nod to him, but Chris, the now-beaten swim god from Southern Catholic, scowls deeply.

Allan had won! His time was relayed by the announcer over and over. He'd beat some kind of national record, and by the sound of it, by half a second! Allan holds up his hand, and the crowd claps a thunderous response.

So goes Allan Westerfield's thirteen to fourteen,

one-hundred-meter freestyle race. He won't get kicked out of school, and to top it off, he's now qualified for the Nationals.

Allan lets the water fall off his swim cap and cascade down his face as he listens to the beating of his heart. He's light headed but so happy. Swimming is his purpose, his reason for living. Allan looks across the sea of happy faces in the bleachers and listens to the clapping.

Allan grabs a towel from his coach—who's as happy as an overfed dolphin—turns, and sits. He's got one more race to win, but any worry or doubt vanishes. He can do it, there's too much on the line.

His mother mouths something to him, her cheeks red from smiling and squealing.

From the entrance walks a slightly crooked man, shorter than average and with a long brown ponytail. His math teacher, Mr. Morgan! *What is he doing here?* The guy was always trying to be cool and hip, but he's so strict no one really likes him.

Mr. Morgan finds the principal sitting in the front row. The two chat as Mr. Morgan shakes his head. The principal waves him off, but Mr. Morgan won't go.

"No," Allan whispers. He knows what's happening. Dread fills Allan's chest like heavy lead balls.

A cascade effect happens, similar to falling dominoes. Mr. Morgan speaks to a referee, who speaks to the judge and recorder, who then scowl and stare. The referee finds Allan's coach, who approaches with a sour face.

"Pack it up," Coach says. "You can't finish the

meet. Get your grades in line and do it again next year. Got it?"

Allan stands, stifling his tears. He notices the principal speaking to his mother, and as her smile collapses into dust, Allan's knees weaken to the point of overcooked spaghetti.

The crowd is still cheering for Allan; some try to catch his eye and wave. They'll hear the news soon. Allan feels the heat of embarrassment hit him head-on and rushes to the dressing room. The quiet, tile-covered room allows his anger to surface. He changes into his blue-and-gray school uniform and slams his locker closed. *Why do I have to know math anyway? None of it matters to me!*

After gathering his things, he leaves, meeting his mother in the hall outside the locker room. His mother's face is different, altered somehow.

She holds up the test Allan failed. Her grip has slightly crumpled the paper. Even still, Allan can clearly see the big red F on the top.

"Boy, you've messed up."

"But—"

"Not another word. I'm ready to blow like a volcano. Let's go." Mrs. Westerfield hisses, keeping her voice as low as possible. She grabs his shirt collar and tugs him toward the oversized mahogany door that leads to the main hallway. "You can't swim with grades like these and you know it."

Allan doesn't say a word. It is true, he knew this day would come. It's calling out the beast in his mother, and no athletic award could ease her anger. He wants to shrink into a tiny marble and roll away or clink down a gutter and into a storm drain where he will be safe.

Mrs. Westerfield practically drags him down the wide hallway. Its walls have accumulated a myriad of awards, photos, and student artwork. He'd won the one-hundred-meter freestyle, so he should get his picture on the wall, but he won't. His math teacher has stripped him of his victory.

"You weren't supposed to race today. You have to have a 3.2 GPA to play sports. You don't have a 3.2 GPA. Do you know what that means?"

Allan shakes his head.

"You're in the best private school in the state. Your father and I aren't paying for you to swim. We're paying for you to learn." For a few moments, the only sound is the clicking of Mrs. Westerfield's heels on the tile floor. "Besides, without that GPA you will be disqualified. All your efforts might go down the drain."

Allan looks at the polished wood-paneled walls of Greenville Academy. He's just won a state competition but will be stripped of his trophy. It will go to that smarmy Chris guy. *How can they do this? I still beat him. It has nothing to do with not turning in some work and failing one little math test.*

Coming to Greenville Academy was supposed to make things better. At first its prestigious austere haunted Allan every time he walked through the towering front doors. Everyone is too smart, too driven, too…something he isn't. Until taking the lead on the swim team, Allan had never felt like he belonged at the academy. They do not want average kids, kids that can't figure out algebra or memorize the periodic table or grasp Latin. He hates Latin. Now he'll be kicked out and have to go back to the public school, which didn't even have a swim team.

Today, the kids that usually ignored him cheered his name. Their parents will talk about him. He is now the fastest swimmer Greenville has ever seen.

"You've never done this before," Mrs. Westerfield hisses. She is normally a lean woman, but her outrage amplifies her muscles and veins. Her hair and eye make-up appear darker in her rage though it is midday and sunny. She's normally very pretty, a good mom. But on occasions like this, she morphs into a surly, fire-breathing troll queen whose cruelty reigns over Allan and his father. Her nails dig into his arm as she pulls him down the steps toward the car that idles at the curb. They feel like claws. "You've never lied to me like this. You are grounded from Mac and your video games for a month, or more. Your father and I haven't quite decided yet. Unless you bring up these grades and fast, you will not swim on any team again. Do you hear me?"

Allan nods. He's shorter than average with light brown hair like his dad, thin with blue eyes like his mom. He's thirteen and a half and keenly aware that his mother is dragging him around like a child. School has been over for a couple of hours, but everyone still in the library can see his humiliation. "Your teacher said you're failing assignments and doodling on everything. She's caught you drawing a six-headed sea creature in a textbook. That's vandalism. You are way better than this." Allan sees troll hair sprouting from under his

Strange Lands

mother's shirtsleeves. "It's not just math. Mr. Morgan just got out of a meeting with your science and your language arts teachers. I just learned that you've flushed a third of your grade by not doing a science project. Why wouldn't you do one? You didn't even tell me you had one this quarter." When Allan doesn't answer, she bends to his eye level. "Answer me or so help me God."

"I, uh—" Tears roll down his face. "I didn't know what to do. Everyone had good ideas but me. I couldn't think of anything."

"Your brain works, I know it does." Mrs. Westerfield opens the car door for Allan, the hunchback growing on her shoulders. The troll queen will eat me alive, Allan thinks. She taps her foot as Allan hops in, and then she slams the door shut. To Allan's horror, his dad is driving.

"What in the hell are you doing? I know you're only in the eighth grade, but if you mess this up, you won't get into an Ivy League school. You can kiss Princeton goodbye." Allan's father clicks the car into gear and pulls into traffic, squealing the tires.

His mother holds up the test. "Allan failed his math midterm. Not a low C or a D. A big fat F. He also missed his science project, but never misses swim practice or his TV shows." Fangs have grown from her distended lower jaw. She snorts. Or did she? Allan rubs his eyes, and his mother looks normal again, though she continues her rant, "Your father could have helped you with math. And you could have asked me for some ideas about your science project. I'm an Ornithologist. What about a project on rare birds? Remember the Yellow Bellied Canaries I studied last year? They turned red in

21

a single generation. They would have made a wonderful science project." She grunts in frustration, something she does when words cannot convey her emotions. The grunt is a good sign, however. It means she's running out of steam.

Allan hopes he can still avoid being her main course. "I'm sorry. I didn't think…" Allan tries to find a piece of fingernail to chew, but they have been chomped away already. He wants to tell his father that Princeton means nothing to him, but Allan bites his tongue. He knows better than to dismiss his father's holy Princeton.

"That's right. You didn't think!" Mr. Westerfield snaps. He changes lanes and yells out the window at a car that zips by. "Watch it! Idiot drivers are everywhere."

"Language, Warren."

"This is your fault, you know. You're the one that read all those crazy kid books by Ricky Boldary to him when he was younger. You know, the ones with those crazy creatures and worlds and Morty's adventures at sea. It messed up his brain. All he thinks about is adventuring and swimming and diving."

"Okay, that makes absolutely no sense," Mrs. Westerfield retorts.

Allan sniffles and wipes his eyes with the back of his hand. He hates himself when he makes his parents mad. He feels stupid, worthless. The science project scared him to death. School scares him. The only thing he really wants to do is swim and go on adventures. He thinks about racing other kids and going to the Olympics. He wants to explore the castles of Europe and hunt for elusive sea creatures and hold the record for the deepest free dive. The Discovery Channel has tons of people that make good money doing that stuff.

Mrs. Westerfield turns to Allan. She takes a deep breath. Her usually tame hair is ruffled and messy. "Look, as you get older school gets harder. You've got to come to us for help. That's what we're here for.

"The world has too many Ricky Boldary wannabes and head-screwed-on-backward athletes. We need scientists and mathematicians. That's where the money is. That's where you'll have a future."

Allan is about to say he won't mess up again, but his mother cuts him off.

"I'm still mad," she says, then turns away looking more tired than ferocious.

"You've got such a powerful drive. Look how you push yourself in the water. Why not push your mind like that? Science is only half academic. The other half is passion, which you have in spades. Just forget about the fantasies for a while. You can always race and dive and explore places; you only have one chance to get middle school right."

Mr. Westerfield wears new leather gloves that have little holes cut around the knuckles. They creak like a rusty hinge when he squeezes the wheel. Traffic is thick, not unusual for this time of day. Allan looks out the window. The sun slips behind a dark cloud. I could do a science project about birds? How boring, Allan thinks. Now if that bird has short razor-sharp teeth, that would be cool.

Movement catches his eye as the car slows to a stop. A beetle with a black shell and an oblong body lands on the edge of the window. Beyond it, a swarm of beetles leap from car to car. Do beetles have parents that yell at them? Do they have homework that makes life difficult and cruel? If given the choice, would that beetle trade its meager life for mine? Allan taps the glass twice where the beetle is. To his surprise, it taps its front leg twice. Allan taps the glass three times. The beetle copies him. His eyes widen, and his breath catches in his chest.

The car starts to move again, sweeping past the swarm of beetles. The one beetle holds on for as long as it can until the wind whips it away. Allan slips out of the top part of the seatbelt and cranes his neck to look out the back windshield so he can see the beetle join the swarm. There are so many. He's never seen a cloud of bugs so thick. It rises over the cars and into the sky like dark smoke.

Suddenly, the car is hit head-on by a much larger vehicle. Airbags explode from the door panels and hammer Allan from the side. His lap belt catches his waist, but his unprotected torso snaps forward. Glass fills the air like confetti and sounds like a million wind chimes. Silence envelops him, and he sees only a bright light. Another car slams into the opposite side and flips the car over. Time slows as the vehicle absorbs the energy of the collision. The roof caves in as easily as crumpling paper. Then Allan blinks out, enveloped in silence.

Chapter 2
New Rules

Allan awoke on a stiff bed wrapped in warm sheets. Something is sticking in his wrist; other things are stuck to his head and a plastic clip is wrapped around his index finger. He sits up quickly. Pain sizzles in his brain until he's forced to sit back down. A strange woman bursts into his room, wearing baby-blue pajamas with little bears printed all over them. Her mouth moves, but Allan can't hear her voice. Seconds passed before he can hear her. It's as if someone has cranked up the volume: beeping machines, someone in the hallway yelling, heavy footfalls.

He looks around. Cartoon covered wallpaper, a side table holding flowers and balloons, a window that's dark behind the blinds, a strange man sleeping in a chair with a magazine lying across his chest and ear buds dangling from his ears. A nurse grabs Allan's hand and squeezes.

"It's okay, hon. Just relax. You're in the hospital. There was an accident, but you're safe now."

Allan's heart threatened to burst out of his chest. He tries to scream, but can't. Another nurse injects a liquid into his IV and instantly Allan relaxes and melts into the bed. His heart slows and his thoughts stop. The beeping in the room sings a lullaby rhythm.

The strange man wakes and bounces out of the chair like he's launched by a huge spring. He takes Allan's other hand. Allan yanks it away, not knowing the man. A sliding glass door opens, and a doctor wearing a long white coat entered.

"It's okay, kid. Doc's gonna check you out." The man has light brown, tousled hair and torn jeans. His eyes look familiar, but a long fuzzy beard hides his face.

The doctor sweeps a flashlight across Allan's eyes. He peers into Allan's mouth and ears and speaks quietly to the nurse. He turns back around and smiles wide.

"Hello, Allan. I'm Doctor Kumar. There is no easy way to say this, but you've been in a coma for two weeks. Try to relax. The bones in your lower spine have shattered, and splinters punctured your spinal cord. We cannot fix your spinal cord. You will probably never walk again." The bearded man grabbed Allan's hand and, this time, Allan didn't pull away.

"I'm your uncle, Rubic," the bearded man says. Allan hasn't seen his uncle in a long time. His thick beard makes him look different. After watching Rubic speak and absorbing his shape and mannerisms, Allan remembers him. He used to see Rubic on Thanksgiving Day. He'd show up with fireworks on the Fourth of July and was always at Allan's birthdays until four years ago when he moved to California. "Your parents died in the crash, kiddo." Rubic's eyes filled with tears then slid down his face.

Allan searches for his parents. *That's not possible.*

His mouth wouldn't open and his head starts spinning. He tries to pull his legs to his chest. When that didn't work, he tries to roll off the bed. The doctor and the bearded man force him back and press him into the mattress. His legs didn't work. Some hard, plastic thing was strapped to his back, keeping him prostrate. He sobs and squeezes his eyelids shut, wishing it all away. Wishing to be in his mother's arms, he sees her in his mind. She is beautiful and strong, but she can't come closer to him. She remains at a distance. *Was she still mad?* She steps away. *No, come back. Help me!* Allan thinks.

Rubic helped the nurse fix the sheet and says, "That's enough bomb shells for today, Doc."

The machines beep out of control and Allan passes out.

Early one morning, the door opens and a nurse enters. In the hallway Rubic is speaking to a thin woman wearing a grey professional suit holding a thick binder. Allan can barely hear Rubic's voice, "Me? Why me? I never agreed to take him. What do I know about caring for a kid who can't use his legs?"

The woman replies, "If not you, there's always foster care." The door clicks shut muting their conversation. Allan squeezed his eyes shut fighting back tears. The nurse said something to him, but he didn't hear her. She fixed his blanket, tucked it under him to ward off the cold and left.

###

It's been eight months since Allan left the hospital. Allan wheels himself around the house with increasing skill. There are dings in the doorframes and dents in the walls, but they are old marks from when Allan first came home from the hospital and had to get used to being stuck in a wheelchair.

Dr. Brooks, still stopping by the house twice a week, sits in the armchair with her note pad. "How does it feel to be using a wheelchair?" She's in her usual gray pantsuit, has dark hair like Allan's mother and has kind blue eyes.

Allan types on his iPad, skipping words and abbreviating, 'sucks. Bump into door frames + chair doesn't fit into bathroom.

"It will get easier," she says, adjusting her glasses. "There will be construction crews out this week or next to fix things. I think your uncle is just waiting for the settlement money."

Money? Allan thinks. *So he's got all my parents' money now.* Allan has always liked his uncle Rubic, but his mother insisted he was lazy and couldn't keep a job. Now Rubic owns the house his father worked so hard to buy. It doesn't seem right, none of it.

The front door opens. Uncle Rubic enters with bags hanging from his fists, a lot of bags. He must be trying to beat the world record for how many bags he can hold at one time.

"Hey, kid. I got pudding cups. Your fav. Some lady at the store wanted the last of them, but I got 'em. She looked at me like I didn't deserve 'em. Like a grown man can't like pudding." He drops the overstuffed plastic bags, digs through one of them and tosses a pudding cup at Allan. "Her snot-nosed kids can do without. You should've seen her cart. It was filled with crap: cupcakes, brownies, pop tarts, a huge bag of sour candies, and boxes of every kind of sugar cereal there was. Her kids are probably all toothless butter balls by now."

Allan opens the pudding and tips it up like a drink. The pudding slowly rolls out of the cup and into his mouth. Dr. Brooks stands. "Well, I think we're done for today."

"Any peep?" Rubic asks as he rips the lid off his pudding and drinks it in the same way.

She shakes her head as she tucks her notes and files into her briefcase. "He doesn't even draw anymore."

"Gotta speak sometime, kid. Doc says your voice is fine."

Rubic and Dr. Brooks move away from Allan so he can't hear them, but he does. He hears a lot of whispering about him these days.

"Yes, his mind won't allow him to speak. It's a coping mechanism. But he'll come around on his own time. Trust that."

Rubic cleans the pudding cup with his finger then licks it. "However long it takes, huh? I know that gets you over here twice a week so you can get that fat paycheck, but I think we oughta try and speed things up a bit."

"Trust me," she says in a hushed voice. "These kinds of cases are textbook. He's got to work through this on his own. He's just now starting to go outside again where people can see him. That's a big step."

"So one day he's just gonna be like, Uncle Rub pass the ketchup would ya?" Rubic shakes his head. "I don't buy it. Gotta try something else."

"I'm a good therapist," she defends.

Rubic rolls his eyes. "Yeah, I got it. And I'm a turkey sandwich."

Dr. Brooks stomps out the front door, letting it close a little harder than necessary. Rubic snaps his fingers. "I know. Hey buddy, do you know what your dad's favorite thing to do was? Well, used to be his favorite thing. Up until his job took over his life."

Allan types on his iPad. 'fishing?'

Rubic karate kicks then punches the air symbolizing his enthusiasm. "That's right. We're gonna go fishing. Forget all these city dwellers. We're going up to the mountains to go catch us some fish." He ruffles Allan's hair.

'no thanks. something bad will happen.'

"Nonsense. That's fear talking. You'll love it. Nothing but fresh air, squirrels and fire. We'll make a big fire. Capital B, capital F."

'have swim practice,' Allan types. Even though he can't race and he doesn't want to be in the water anymore, Rubic and his therapist make him go. Allan is all too aware that he will never hear the roar of the crowd again. He'll never see an opponent fall behind, and he'll never get another chance to get an award hung on the hall of fame at Greenville.

"They won't miss you. No excuse can save you this time. You used to want to be an explorer, or was it a sea captain? Remember that? Just like that kid in those books, your mom would read to you. What was it called? Ah yeah, Morty's Travels." Allan looks away. Rubic shrugs, "Well, either way, we're going, and I think you'll dig it once we get up there."

'can't run away so no choice. never have choice.' Rubic doesn't see the text, so Allan deletes it. He rolls to the window and stares into the daylight. It hurts his eyes at first. People pass by wearing headphones or chatting on their telephones. He sees a woman running with her dog. The muscles in her calves tighten and flex. He hopes she falls, sprains her ankle or skins her knee. Everyone is wearing shorts. There's another runner and then a walker. The more the person is exercising, the less clothing they wear, like they're taunting Allan with their healthy bodies, rubbing it in his face.

A delivery truck rumbles by, startling Allan. Everything startles him these days. The world is filled with dangerous things: things that crash into you, steal your life and your parents, and make you hurt all over. No! Allan does not want to go camping. In fact, he doesn't want to leave his house ever again.

Friday finally arrives. Allan hopes Rubic will ditch this camping idea. You can't camp if you can't walk.

After burnt scrambled eggs and watery orange juice, Rubic presses the button on Allan's iPad that shuts down the video game. Allan scowls.

"Time to go camping. I know you don't want to, but trust me. It'll be good." Rubic loads his truck then comes back inside to get Allan. He carries Allan to his pickup truck while Allan protests with silence and frowns. The back is piled high with camping gear and covered with a blue tarp. He sits Allan in the passenger seat.

'not bringing my chair?' Allan types.

"Nah, you can't roll that thing in the dirt. I'll carry you. And I've got camping chairs, hammocks and a couple of air mattresses. It'll be great."

'want chair.'

Rubic puts his hands on his hips and thinks for a millisecond. "Fine, if you insist. I guess it's your new baby blanket now. Don't get too used to it, though. There's a chance you could walk again. Doc says we should try seeing a different specialist." He loads the chair under the tarp then hops in the truck.

'can't breathe.' Allan types. He clutches his chest and drops his chin as panic seizes his heart and thickens his blood. Dizziness adds dark shapes to his vision as though death is doing laps around his head, waiting for him to die. Rubic unzips a bag in between them. "Here, kid. You're just nervous about driving. Doc said you'd be like this for a while. Take this. It'll relax you."

Allan takes the pill. Like the flip of a switch, he relaxes quickly. The pill didn't even have time to hit his stomach.

On the road, the traffic is bad. Rubic cusses at the other drivers just like Allan's father used to. They sound so similar sometimes. Tears swell up in Allan's eyes.

Once Rubic gets to the freeway, he seems to relax. "We're goin' to the river me and your dad used to fish when we were your age. It's perfect. No idiot drivers, no fools lookin' for a hand out, no alarm clocks. There's just the big ball of light in the sky and those hungry fish."

Allan ignores Rubic. And he feels justified. If he's going to be dragged out of his house, he doesn't have to play nice. He flips his texting program off. With a tap on the screen, a video game loads and he resumes his previous game. It's some little character jumping and throwing weapons and ducking and dodging. He compiles millions of coins and passes level after level with increasing skill.

During the drive, Allan misses how the city shrinks and thins like a sandcastle being washed out by the waves. Instead of corner drugstores, fancy restaurants, and gum-laden sidewalks, there are trees, small homes and a passing freight train. He doesn't see any of it. Instead, his little character misses a platform and is impaled on spikes. Its body flashes and dissolves and the level starts over. Not a scratch, not a bruise. Allan wishes he would flash and dissolve so he could try his life again.

After four hours of driving, Rubic hits a dirt road, and the ride gets bumpy. The trees, much bigger, stand straight like soldiers. The air thins and is cold. Rocks push out of the dry pine needles like giant monuments, and dust clings to the windows, sneaking through the A/C vents. The road narrows until there is only one lane. Allan finally looks out the window. He stares into the forest as it passes by. It's ugly and boring, he thinks. It's dirty and filled with dangerous animals. There's nothing out there for me, nothing.

Half an hour later, Rubic parks under a gigantic tree. "We're here." There are no facilities, no tables, and no trashcans. "This is camping. We're out in the middle of nowhere living like the cavemen did." He laughs. "Not really. I've got everything we need. I'll teach you how to fish and tie a bowline. And you can carve something out of wood. How does that sound?"

Allan fakes a wide smile. He doesn't smile much these days, so the stretching of his cheeks feels tight. Sadness swarms like whispering ghosts and he wants more medicine. He wants his father with them.

Rubic puts his hand on Allan's shoulder. "It's okay, kid. You want him to be here. I know. So do I. He's the only dude in the whole world that I could stand. But a part of him is here. There are other worlds besides our own. He's up there watchin' us, hoping you'll try to have a good time."

Rubic sets up the tent and table and then gathers some firewood and lights the fire. "You've got new rules to live by, kid, but you're still in the game." He's a skillful camper and is done as the sky darkens. In silence, the two eat hotdogs and stare at the fire.

Chapter 3
The True Story

Rubic hands Allan a mug of hot chocolate.

'not thirsty' Allan types on his iPad. He feels the dark night press on his back, the fire his only source of comfort.

Rubic huffs. "Since when do you have to be thirsty to drink hot cocoa?" He tries to hand it over to Allan again. "It has little marshmallows."

Allan takes the mug without looking away from the camp fire. He feels connected to the flames, to the heat, to the tiny burning city of coals.

At one point in his life, he wanted to be an adventurer and discover something no one had ever found, like a new species or a faraway tribe. Now, he's stuck in a wheelchair for the rest of his life. That means no adventuring for him, no swimming or diving. His dreams and aspirations have vanished, leaving behind only ghosts in his head.

Allan notices Rubic staring at him. The lingering moment stretches out, illuminating the vast emotional distance between them. Finally, Rubic says, "Am I that boring to be around?"

Allan types quickly. 'no. you adult, me teen. adults might be from earth but teens from alpha centauri.'

Rubic nods. "I see. We might as well be speaking different languages." Rubic sighs and pats Allan on the shoulder.

'plus, you're kind of funny lookin' Allan types. He smiles, but only half a smile.

Rubic chuckles.

'how bout a scary story?' Allan suggests.

Rubic's eyes widen. "Okay, but I gotta warn you. This is a true story." Rubic sips from his steaming mug and then clears his throat. "Have you ever heard of a Shadic?"

Allan shakes his head.

Rubic stares at the glowing fire, turning the cup of cocoa in circles. The wind whistles through the trees and disturbs the fire as if anticipating the story. "Years ago I was camping out here with your dad. We were sitting around the campfire, just like we are now when an old man came out of the dark. He was as old as a man can get, his hair white as spider's silk. He wore a cloak that looked as old as time itself. Sewn patchworks of every color kept it together, keeping it from falling off his bony shoulders. He sat on a log near us and didn't say a word. He had a flower in his hand, a big one, and a sack slung over his shoulder. We didn't say anything at first, but then I asked him his name. He looked at me and said it didn't matter because he will be dead soon."

Allan listens intently, noticing Rubic's fidgeting.

"Your dad asked the man if he was okay, but he didn't answer. He told us he had traveled across the galaxy, running for his life from Shadic Rulers. Shadics were the most powerful creatures the Galaxy had ever known. They were so strong they could leap a dozen feet in the air. They had razor-sharp beaks like birds, red eyes like the belly of a volcano, and spikes that covered their bodies and dripped a kind of poison. They were intelligent, too, and were collecting scientists and secrets that could give them eternal life and control over worlds."

Allan gasps ever so quietly.

"The ol' man said he knew of an insect, a beetle that would give anyone immortal life. Imagine living forever." Rubic smiled and then continued. "He also said that Earth was in danger. If the Shadic race obtained the secret of immortality, an army of the most brutal rulers would come to our planet and take it over."

Allan rolls his eyes. 'thought this was true story. That's just science fiction.'

"No, this is true. I don't know how the guy traveled across space, he didn't have a ship or anything, but I really did meet him up here. If you think there aren't other worlds out there, your eyes aren't open enough. Now let me continue." He sips. "The old man confessed that he had told one Shadic, I can't remember the name he gave me, the secret of the immortality beetle. But it was the only way to escape Lan Darr. He was so ashamed of his weakness and was on the run ever since.

"Fifty years passed until another clan of Shadic rulers caught up with him. He refused to give the knowledge over. The old man lifted his sleeve and exposed a whole bunch of scars across his arms. He said his entire body was covered. He escaped them because he convinced them he would show them the planet that had the beetle. I could tell, he was still on the run. Boy, it freaked me out. The worst company to have is the guy that is being hunted. Too easy to be collateral damage, you know?"

Rubic finishes the hot cocoa and sets the cup between his feet and then shoves his hands deep into his pockets. "Your dad gave the man something to eat and drink. When the ol' man was done, he stood, thanked us, and headed into the dark without a flashlight. We noticed he didn't even have shoes. Your dad and me stared at each other, wondering what we should do.

"A screech tore through the quiet night. The shrill sound vibrated my bones and lit every nerve in my body. It wasn't any kind of sound we'd ever heard before and not of this planet, for sure. Then, suddenly, the tallest of the trees exploded. We fell to the ground and covered our heads. Leaves and sticks rained down on us. We heard the old man scream. Your dad jumped up first and pulled his flashlight out of his pocket and ran off toward the man. He said we needed to help him because it was the right thing to do. I followed with my flashlight.

"Your dad stopped not even two hundred yards away, next to a large tree. I caught up with him, flinging my light everywhere. The tree was covered in blood, a lot of blood. And there was an 'X' carved into the side, burned black and smoking. The old man's travel sack lay at the base of the tree next to that large flower he'd been holding, and that was it." Rubic looks around, acting overly cautious. The firelight catches only the edges of his facial features and his bushy beard. Shadows deepen the look of his eye sockets and mouth. "The woods were alive with alien sounds. Our flashlights suddenly went out. Dozens of red glowing eyes were around us. They watched with fiery intensity and then moved closer, tightening the trap. I panicked. Your father panicked. We ran so hard we didn't have time to look behind us, but we could hear them coming, crashing through the brush and snapping branches. The truck was close and unlocked, thank God. We leaped into the cab through the driver door and scrambled to get our feet inside. I saw a dozen dark shapes coming fast, but I slammed the door shut. Your dad tossed the keys at me, and I fired up the engine just as one of 'em landed in the back, bouncing us like it was as heavy as a half-ton boulder. I fired up the engine and hit the gas. The Shadic flew off.

"I didn't stop, just kept going, leavin' all our gear behind. We called the cops and reported the incident, but they never found the old man's body. We knew we'd seen one of the Shadics the old man was talking about and if we didn't get to our truck as fast as we did, we'd have been killed too."

Allan feels a shiver inch up his back, and his hair stand on end. The darkness around the campfire had just gotten a little darker. Rubic continues the scary story, "If anyone asks me if I believe in aliens, I say, yes. Not only do I believe in them, I was only a few feet away when one of them killed an old man. Splattered him across the trunk of a pine tree then marked its kill like it was keeping score. You think that nothin' scares me, well, Shadics do."

Allan grabs his iPad. 'not true. i not scared.'

The yellow firelight reflects across Rubic's wide eyes. "Oh, it's true. There are other worlds with histories and intelligence and brutality. One day, we'll meet them. I just hope it's on our terms."

A creak and a bang break the private bubble around Allan and Rubic. Something comes from the dark toward the campfire, for real! It moves like a cheetah, leaping over a log, getting closer and closer. It's dark, like a shadow, with two glowing eyes.

Allan's eyes and mouth open up. He shields his face from whatever is coming for them. If he could speak, he would have screamed. Rubic falls over backwards in his chair and lands hard, screaming loud and long for the both of them.

The attack will come any minute. Allan braces for the sharp teeth and the pain of death. But instead, he feels a warm, slobbery lick.

Allan opens his eyes, barely able to see due to the thundering beat of his heart. A large dog, furry and brown with a black patch over one eye, sits next to him licking his elbow. Its tail wags and the firelight reflects across its kind eyes.

Rubic gets to his knees. "Holy Mother of all things. That really had me spooked." He laughs. "I was so startled. I thought I was going to pop like a balloon."

A woman approaches from the darkness, her boots treading softly on the pine needles. She wears a green wildlife management uniform that is too tight for her large chest. Allan imagines the buttons flying off and taking out his eye.

"Hello campers," she says.

Rubic looks shocked and confused. "Hey. Uh, is there a problem?"

"I'm Alice. I've got some bad news. This isn't a sanctioned campsite, and fires are forbidden this time of year."

"I thought this was a free country. I need to grease your palms, do I?" Rubic stands, folds his arms and narrows his eyes. It is his tough, don't-mess-with-me face.

The woman's smile turns down. "Put the fire out. You've got 'til noon tomorrow to leave unless you want a hefty fine. I'm sorry, but some places are off-limits to civilians." She whistles and her dog follows her to her truck, which was so far away, it was almost as if she intended to startle them.

"Well, I'll be a monkey's uncle. No one has ever kicked me off this mountain."

Allan types, 'can try fishing some other time.'

"Yeah, right. You heard me. This is a free country. We're not going anywhere. It's our God-given right to go camping anywhere we want." Rubic grabs a handful of pine needles and sniffs them. "Smells like free pine needles to me." He chuckles and drops them.

Rubic whistles the "Star Spangled Banner."

Great. My uncle's a hipster hick, Allan thinks. How is my father even related to this guy?

"We'll put out the fire, though. I don't want to burn the forest down. Then we'll hit the sack."

At five o'clock in the morning, Rubic shakes Allan awake. "Hey kid, the early bird gets the worm then uses that worm to hook the fish. Get up."

Allan reaches for his iPad. He types, 'no. too tired. miss my mom and dad.'

"Damn it, Allan! Look, you're not the only one that lost someone. I lost my brother. I introduced your parents. I've lost my life too. Like I know how to take care of a paraplegic. I can't even cook eggs." Rubic's face is red and hard as petrified wood. Then he looks away. "Would you rather me put you into foster care? Huh? 'Cause that would make it real easy for me. Then you can mope behind the same four walls for the rest of your life, always thinking about what could've been."

Allan wipes tears away and sniffles. 'fine,' he types. 'bathroom first.'

Rubic sighs. He wonders if this is a good idea. Maybe Allan isn't ready to be pushed. He sits on his sleeping bag, scratching his beard. "This is a waste of time."

Allan shakes his head. 'I'll fish. show me.'

Rubic doesn't budge.

'please.'

"Fine, but you're going to have to try. Really try." Rubic helps Allan slide his useless legs into pants, then tugs on socks and shoes. Allan's face is hard, his frown deep. "It's okay. I don't mind helping you get dressed. Not a big deal. We're family."

Allan swallows the lump in his throat and grinds his teeth. He's embarrassed that Rubic sees him in his boxers. Only Allan's mother could make him feel comfortable in these situations. Rubic hauls Allan by his armpits to a bush behind the tent where Allan pees.

After setting Allan in his wheelchair, Rubic equips himself with fishing gear: a brimmed hat decorated with a bear pin, fish pins and a pin of a woman in a red swimsuit, and a tan vest with a handful of pockets. He pauses a moment and looks at Allan who is watching him. Rubic unsnaps the pin of the woman in the red swimsuit and pins it on Allan's shirt. "There. Your dad gave me this one. He knows how much I love old 50's pin-up girls."

Allan isn't sure what to think. He touches the pin. It's smooth metal with glossy red paint where the swimsuit is. The woman has a slender, busty figure, and her legs are slightly crossed. The bathing suit is a one-piece suit, and she has long curly blond hair. He's sure his mother would not approve but keeps it right where Rubic pinned it knowing that his dad would approve.

Rubic forces Allan's wheelchair over the pine needles and rocks to the river. He spins Allan around and drags the chair into the rocky-bottom river, moving slowly so as not to disturb the fish. The water soaks Allan's shoes and jeans, but it doesn't matter. He's a paraplegic now, so wet shoes mean nothing anymore. If you ask him, he doesn't belong on a secluded mountain, between tall canyon walls, and in a river trying to fish like a normal boy.

The river is the width of a two-lane road and around two feet deep. According to Rubic, it's filled with fish because no one ever comes up to this part of the mountain. The roads leading to the campsite are dirt, the pine trees as tall and dense as they get, and there are no showers or toilets or trailer home hookups.

"Getting far away from it all is the only way to escape the jerks in the cities," Rubic had said on the bumpy drive up the mountain. Allan had thought about pointing out the fact that the back of the truck was filled with camping chairs, tables, air mattresses, a stove, lanterns and other comforts, but didn't say a word. He couldn't speak; after all, his voice doesn't work anymore.

Rubic pulls Allan's chair to the middle of the river and locks the wheels. The tires settle into the small, smooth rocks an inch or so. "Don't worry about your chair getting' wet. It's stainless steel and aluminum. Besides, you've gotta get in the water to fish a river." Rubic shows Allan how to tie the hook to the line, where to secure the weight and how to impale the worm on the hook. "It's gross, but you get used to it. Remember the end game. Fresh worms catch the biggest fish."

Rubic casts into the river then reels the line in. He does it over and over then lets Allan try. Allan's cast sends the hook wild. It whips around and zings above Rubic's head.

"Whoa." Rubic ducks. "Don't worry about it. Everyone has trouble casting when they first try. You should've seen your father. He was terrible at it. But before I knew it, he was catching fish bigger than mine." Allan moves his fingers in the air wanting to type a note.

"Sorry kid. No iPad out here. I didn't want it to get wet. Just try and talk to me. Try and use your voice. Doc says there's nothin' wrong with your vocal cords." Rubic waits, but Allan doesn't say anything. He sighs then lets Allan return to casting. "You know, it's amazing what our brain is capable of if we only give it a chance. We

44

can think anything we want. We may not be able to change the bad things that happen, but we can change how we react to 'em. And if you want to talk again you have to start tellin' your brain to do it. You can heal yourself, buddy, if you only try. We are all in the gutter, but some of us are looking at the stars. Some guy named Oscar Wilde said that."

Allan feels bored already. He casts the worm into the river again and sighs. He doesn't get any nibbles and can't even see the fish. He should be here, standing on two legs, with his father. He reels the hook and worm back to the fishing pole and casts the hook far downstream.

A rumble, like the bass of a large speaker blasting low frequencies, shakes the ground and disturbs the mostly placid river. Overhead, the birds leap into the air and flutter away in panic. The snapping and cracking of trees echoes between the canyon walls. Allan and Rubic slowly turn to look upriver. The rumble grows louder and louder. A wall of water appears and crashes toward them. It looks like the teeth of a giant machine lashing out, crunching all that gets in its way. Trees fall, boulders slam into each other, and branches as sharp as spears fly downstream. Rubic hoists Allan out of his chair and runs. The water slows him, holding on to his legs like a million little hands. Just before they get out of the river the water hits them.

Rubic's feet sweep out from under him, and he drops Allan. The water sucks them in, rolling them around in its muddy, frothy wake. Something sharp hits Allan's side. He opens his eyes, but the water stings them.

He sees his uncle's body and reaches out. Rubic grabs his hand. The two are swept over a cluster of boulders, and they fall down a waterfall. Rocks and boulders and debris, bound together by the force of the flood, chase them.

Silence surrounds Allan. He closes his eyes and rolls in the churning wake. It feels like he is dying, but it's an illusion. His senses shut off, and his life force gathers around the vital parts of his body. He's close to death, but not close enough. He has felt this before, on the day he lost the use of his legs.

Strange Lands

Chapter 4
Of Dreams We Travel

Allan's eyes pop open. He's alive! The pine trees tower over his head and a raven sits on a branch cawing at him. Probably waiting for him to die. He realizes he's been unconscious.

Allan pulls his torso out of the mud. Dizziness swims through his brain but settles. It's bright. The sunlight hurts his eyes. Rubic! Allan turns and sees his uncle lying face up ten feet away.

Allan scoots through the muck and reaches Rubic. He grabs his uncle's hand and squeezes, his mind screaming, no, Rubic. Don't be dead. Allan listens for a heartbeat. At first, he doesn't hear one, but then it comes. It's slow and uneven. Tears burst out of Allan as he shakes Rubic, trying to wake him. Rubic doesn't wake. But is he breathing? He isn't.

Panic swarms through Allan as if his veins are filled with tiny piranhas. In swim class, Allan was taught how to get someone breathing if their lungs were full of water. He has to roll Rubic on his side. If that doesn't work, he'll have to start chest compressions. He tries to turn his uncle, but the boulder has pinned Rubic's arm and a part of his chest. He pulls and pulls and pulls harder. Breathe! His mind roars. Allan thrusts his arm under Rubic then dredges out mud and small rocks. His finger jams on a stone, sending pain signals into his overwhelmed brain. The stone is too big to dig up, but he tries again. His fingers slip off it. Rubic's torso is heavy and sinks into the mud. Allan isn't strong enough. He pulls on Rubic's free arm to no effect. Without legs and the leverage, it's hopeless.

Allan starts to pound on Rubic's chest. Water leaks out and he gurgles. Come on Uncle! Allan tips Rubic's head to the side, and more water spills out of Rubic's mouth. He begins breathing. Allan sits back and gasps. Water drips from his hair and stings his eyes. Or is it sweat? Allan shakes Rubic, but he doesn't wake up. Blood coming from Rubic's crushed arm runs into the water. Allan knows he needs to get help. He shakes Rubic again. Get up! Get up! Get up! The sun peeks over the nearby peak, but being wet makes him shiver.

Allan cries. He's got to get help, but he can't walk. He's helpless, weak. He couldn't save his parents, and now he'll watch his uncle die. He's alone now, worse than before. He touches Rubic's beard and wonders how his parents died. Was it painful for them? Allan touches his own face. Maybe his mother got to touch him one last time. Tears blur the light. The life he faces now will be filled with total strangers. He'll be unconnected and unloved. Something twisted and evil came for Allan the day of the car crash. It was death, and it wanted more than his parents, more than Allan's legs. Did it want his uncle now? Maybe it wants him.

Rubic lies pressed into the mud by a large boulder. The cool water rushes by him keeping him wet. His skin looks pale.

No! I can't let this happen. The river isn't very deep here. I can do something. Allan screams inside. He reaches the riverbank and collects rocks and sticks. As the sun makes its way through the sky, Allan builds a dam around Rubic. When he is finished, the water is diverted away from his uncle so he won't freeze in the cold mountain water. The next step is to get help. Allan has to get back to camp. There's a cell phone there; there has to be. Allan takes a deep breath and rolls into the water then lifts himself up. The water isn't moving very fast, but it has strength. It lifts Allan's body as he pulls himself across. At the other side, he drags himself out of the water. He's still small and thin, but his arms are strong from being a powerful swimmer. He sits up and pushes himself backward. He turns his head to see where he's going and then continues scooting backward.

Grass and leaves swipe Allan's arms as he scoots along. The vegetation wipes off the mud that has dried on his skin. On closer inspection, he sees that it's not mud. It's a little pink, and there's a metallic smell to it. He scratches a glob of the goop off his forearm. It's something else, something foul. The trees are caked with the pink stuff as well. Allan uses his hand to clean a wide swath off a nearby tree trunk. The trunk is white underneath. He continues to remove the substance from the trunk. The flood has brought some foul chemical with it.

Allan flips onto his belly. Dr. Jenny, his spirited physical therapist, showed him how to crawl on his knees, but he'd never bothered to practice. Now it seems that might be an alternative way to move. Allan pulls himself onto his knees. He picks up his left hip and leans forward on his arms. His limp, but heavy leg falls forward. He puts his weight on the knee. Then he picks up his right hip and lets it fall forward before returning the weight to it. In this manner, he begins to crawl forward slowly. Sweat drips off his forehead like his head is a rain cloud.

If only he'd eaten this morning. There's no protein bar, snack or drink in his pockets. They're all in the pockets of his wheelchair. In desperation, he bends down and drinks from a puddle. It tastes bad, sharp, and stings the back of his throat, but it's still water. So he drinks again and then rests on his belly.

After crawling up a small slope, Allan rolls onto his back. He's tired. His eyes burn. He can't do this. He's going to die along with his uncle. Will he be able to walk in heaven? Or will God provide a solid gold, diamond-studded wheelchair? Allan giggles at the thought of God sitting on his throne, "Can't use your legs in heaven, but, hey, you don't need them. You've got angel wings." Allan laughs harder. He sees himself fluttering around on little wings as his legs flop like overcooked spaghetti. He can't stop laughing. Head-splitting laughs roll out of his chest until his head thumps.

After what seems like hours, but is only seconds, Allan settles down. He sits up and pushes his torso backward. He wonders why the image of little angel's wings on his back is so funny.

Without explanation, Allan's thoughts move on. He notices his vision has blurred a little. Then he notices patterns dancing in the pine needles. They look like little skeletons locking arms and turning around and around in a macabre kind of line dance. All the pine needles look like this and then the pattern changes.

Allan sees a bug lying on its back in front of him. He flips it over so its wings can fold out of its shell. As it flies away, it leaves a trail behind it like one of those propeller planes that drags banners through the air. Allan rubs his eyes. Why am I seeing things?

He pushes through a thick fern entangled by some type of parasitic plant that wraps around the ferns. On the other side is the largest, most beautiful flower he has ever seen. It has hundreds of tiny blue petals surrounding an orb of light blue fur. He guesses the fur is pollen. The bulb is about as round as a softball. There are patterns in the pollen, and Allan is transfixed for a moment. The petals that encircle the pollen bud twitch as if the flower doesn't like being stared at. Allan smells the flower hoping for a perfume smell, but instead sneezes. Pollen goes everywhere. He sees sparks in the cloud of pollen. Miniature fireworks pop off all around him. His body wretches and he sneezes again. He drops the strange flower, wondering why he is so allergic to it. He usually doesn't have to worry about allergies. He continues to sneeze repeatedly and feels like he's about to pass out. He can't pass out. He can't. The fireworks multiply and rain down on him. They seem to bend the daylight beyond like a lens.

Pain tears through Allan's body. He feels stretched and twisted, squeezed in a giant hand. As quick as the pain comes on, it vanishes. The colors around him change, and so does the foliage. Bird songs, cricket chirps and a faraway hoot have never sounded so unusual, so alien. The flower he'd dropped no longer sits at his side. It's gone, along with that fern. A different kind of plant surrounds him. It isn't green, but teal. Dark red veins twist through the leaves as if it's riddled with an infection.

He looks around, wanting to continue toward camp, but which way does he go? The ground is no longer littered with pine needles. Instead, he's on a thin marbled moss. The trees are thinner and have circular shapes on the trunks instead of crackled bark. Where's camp? He glances around feeling dizzy. Keep going. I need to keep going. If I was crawling in the right direction before, then I'll need to continue that way. I'll run into the road if it even exists anymore. Allan feels shaky and nervous and squeezes his eyes shut.

Allan looks up, startled by black shapes speeding across the forest floor. They wisp by him and leap over rocks and bushes. He can't focus on them, but they look like deer. One comes right at Allan, and he flinches. The thing stops a few feet away. Its shape is reminiscent of a deer, only not solid and more like smoke. Allan should feel afraid but instead feels peace come to him. The deer-like shape comes close to him, and he reaches out to touch it. The smoky deer's snout doesn't touch Allan's skin but flows over his fingers. Allan instantly knows what it is. It's called a Dream Spirit.

Allan hears its voice. It's a soft lilting sound, whispers on the wind. No, not on the wind, Allan can hear it in his head like it's one of his thoughts. You can't be real, Allan thinks. The Dream Spirit's eyes widen showing a white expanse inside its head, contradicting its shadowy form. There's a whole world in there. Its voice warms Allan's muscles and calms his nerves.

It says, "I will give you strength. You are on a noble path, and you will succeed. Ignore the things that haunt you. Push ahead, boy from Earth. The future is a birthing star, and always will be, for the star is ever growing, ever changing. That is the power of now. Go. Save your Uncle."

Something causes the deer-like Dream Spirit to look up and dash away. Allan watches the rest of the stampede pass by. He's left speechless and in awe. That couldn't have been real, could it? I . . . I am dreaming. Wake up, wake up!

Allan squeezes his eyes shut. He wants to continue, but he's so scared. For the few moments, the Dream Spirit was with him, he was safe. Now, he's alone and something strange is happening to him.

Allan lies down. His cheeks rest on the dry needles and the fallen leaves. He wants to continue, to save Rubic. But how?

Strange Lands

Chapter 5
Following Cake

As Allan lies on the forest floor, sweat soaked and aching, he remembers what Rubic had said the day he left the hospital. "Come on kid, home is better than this place. You'll see. I've filled the entire refrigerator up with ice cream."

Rubic had filled the refrigerator up with all different kinds of ice cream. He'd tried so hard. Allan will try, too. He sits up and keeps heading uphill, hopefully toward camp.

Thunder booms overhead. Allan looks up to find that dark clouds have rolled over the blue sky. Lightning flashes. *Just what I need, more water and mud.* Allan drags himself under a colossal, fallen tree trunk. He scoots up another incline. As he pushes through a bush with purple leaves in the shape of W's, he notices a trail. It's just what he has been looking for. He presses his cheek to the dirt on the trail, thankful that there will be no more crawling through strange plants and over sharp rocks. Allan hears his dad's voice in his head: "There is a path to all things good. Follow good things and you'll never need a map."

If the path doesn't lead to camp, Allan figures that it should lead somewhere where he can get help. He's getting good at scooting backward, crawling on his knees and hopping on his hips.

"Oh, scanta landra panta pong. Beautiful pinta pom." Sings a strange high-pitched voice. The song is in a different language, but that doesn't matter. Allan's expectations lift to the tops of the trees. Here comes someone that will help. From behind a tall fern steps something other than a human. But it's not entirely an animal. It is something of a mix. It has the head of a salamander but the body of a man. The thing wears a threadbare gray jacket more suitable to a homeless man than an amphibian. Its glossy black skin looks almost slimy. Its eyes are large, and its pupils are vertical like a viper's.

"The dina is good, the dina is great. The more I serve, the more money I make." it sings this time in English. It carries a large tray with a cake surrounded by purple grapes as big as golf balls. A twig with a leaf sticks out of the cake, but the salamander-man doesn't bother cleaning it off. He struts by Allan without noticing him. Allan rubs his eyes. *Why didn't it see me? This is nuts! I must be hallucinating.* The thing continues around a large outcropping of rock. Allan doesn't see anything scary about the thing. In fact, it looks quite domesticated. And, well, it carries cake. That's not only a good sign; it's a miracle. After all, it's probably some guy in a costume. *Yes, it's just some dude in a funny costume.*

Allan pauses. What if he's wrong? What if the person is bad? Just like a bully can trick you with a smile

and a wink. Life itself seems intent on delivering Allan pain and sorrow and nothing more, so how can he trust anyone or anything?

The image of the tall cake tips his decision. The salamander-man will save him and Rubic. Allan follows the salamander-man, but he can't go fast enough. After Allan rounds the rocky outcropping, there is another twist in the trail that cuts through large trees. The salamander-man is too far ahead. Allan scoots and hops. His palms ache and his muscles shake, but he must catch up.

Come back salamander-man!

Allan opens his mouth. Nothing comes out. His arm gives out, and he falls to his back. He waited too long. Indecision has cost him. On occasion, Allan's father would get impatient with his indecisiveness. He advised Allan to choose, or life would pass him by. Even his mother told him that irrational fear led to indecision.

Allan pounds the dirt. Why does it always take him so long to decide? Indecision is why he didn't complete that science project. Indecision was why his parents were mad at him and why they crashed their car. Snot and tears run down his face.

Allan pulls himself up and starts scooting. A squeal turns his attention to his hands. He lifts it to find a small creature smashed into the mud. The creature squeals again, a painful sound. It has a small head, no bigger than a gumball and a snout like a frog. Its neck is long, and its body is covered in scales. Little horns adorn its head like a mohawk, and it can almost be a large lizard, but it isn't. Its body is more like a human's, just like the salamander-man. Allan picks the sad creature up. It cries out, and Allan drops it. He's never seen anything like it.

From the shadows of the purple plant come a dozen creatures of similar form. They attack Allan by grabbing, hitting and biting. It doesn't hurt, but they still try. Scowls mark their faces, and angry shrieks color their yells.

Get off me! Allan thinks as one biter draws blood from his forearm. He bats one away and scowls the evilest scowl he can muster. The small creatures flee in a panic, their hurt comrade in tow.

If this is my imagination, then I'm not even awake. I must be lying in that stream, unconscious or even dead. Maybe this is the afterlife. Allan looks around. I do have an amazing imagination. My parents and teachers always said so. Just like in class, when Allan tries to concentrate, his brain switches to his drawings instead of paying attention. He's good at imagining odd things. It seems most likely he is still next to his uncle lying unconscious in the riverbed.

Allan laughs and continues crawling, satisfied that his mind is the culprit of all the strangeness. He has to stay focused. No matter how tired he gets, he has to keep going. Dream or not, he's got a job to do.

Chapter 6
Tea Party Rumors

Allan pursues the salamander-man, his best option. He follows the trail through the dense forest, the trees on either side towering over him like skyscrapers.

The daylight darkens, leaving twilight in its wake, and a fog creeps in. Dark clouds crowd the sky above; lightning flickers but it does not rain. Not yet.

Voices snap him out of his thoughts. The fog has obscured the trail completely. Allan drags himself toward the voices and peeks around a tree. Forty feet away is a table and chairs and sitting at the table are two smaller salamander-people. They, too, have shiny black skin. One has orange spots on its neck and head; the other has yellow markings. They're wearing the funniest clothes. One has a collar of towering petals; the other's collar is made of wires with colorful balls at the ends. They laugh and sip from teacups. The taller salamander-man with the suit cuts the cake into slices and serves each salamander-person.

The orange-marked salamander-person shovels a large bite of cake into its mouth and licks its lips with a long black tongue. "Oh, ho-ho. This is good. I'm enjoying this vacation though I cannot see a thing now that the fog is in and the day is leaving." It takes a fork and reaches for the cake. The fork lands off to the side, clinking on the plate. "Oh, ho ho. I just had you cake, now where have you gone?"

"The cake is good, but the tea is better. Can you acquire a sugar cube for me please?" The yellow-marked salamander-person asks. It fumbles for a teacup, bumps the cup then catches it, but not before spilling half the tea on the table. The spilled tea releases steam into the air. "Pardon me," the yellow one apologizes then lifts the cup and holds it closer to its friend.

The orange one reaches out blindly and searches the table until it finds the plate of sugar cubes. It tries to drop a cube in the other's cup, but the cube hits the lip, falls off the side and rolls off the table. Neither creature notices.

"Thank you." The yellow one sips from the cup. "That sugar cube is just what the tea needed." It sips again. "Though I might need one more."

"You're so welcome. Now where is that cake?" The orange one fumbles with its fork, but can't find anything.

Allan feels like laughing because he can't believe his eyes or his ears.

The orange salamander-person finds the cake and crams a bite into its mouth. "Have you heard the bad news?"

"Oh my, what now? Has the testing gone terribly wrong again? Has someone passed on?"

"No, but Jibbawk struck again this week. Killed three Lan Darrians this time. Oh, the poor souls. It leaves 'X' scratch marks on the trees. The 'X' marks bleed. Oh, I shiver to think of it. It just won't leave us alone."

"It's been killing our people for fifty years now. It will never leave us be."

"But our energy crystals." The orange salamander touched a glowing stone on the table. "The crystals protect us. Its light is too bright for Jibbawk."

"The crystals have worked for many years, but they don't last forever, and we've not found any more in the Melda Mines," says the yellow one.

"For now, ours is bright. We might not be able to have these little tea parties when our crystal runs out." The orange one shudders. "The Jibbawk wants revenge only. He's a Shadic immortal you know. There's no way to kill Jibbawk."

Rubic had told him a story about Shadics, but Allan had thought it had just been made up to scare him. If these salamander-people are real, then maybe Shadics were real too. Maybe this Shadic Jibbawk is in these woods, hunting Lan Darrians. Allan makes a noise that sounds like a peep. The salamander-people look in his direction. Though they cannot see, they know he is there.

"Who's there?" The orange one cries, its eyes open wide. "Oh, it is Jibbawk. I just know it!"

"Roggy will protect us."

"We have cake," the orange one says, looking back and forth, as blind as a rock.

From the fog, Allan sees a head pop up. It is a furry, shaggy head with large floppy ears. It has a dog snout with large jowls and thick, sharp teeth. It growls then leaps and gallops toward Allan. It slides in the moss and stops just inches from Allan's face. Another peep comes from his mouth as fear hits him over the head with the force of a sledgehammer. The dog speaks. "What is this? A human boy?"

"Oh my! How did a boy get out here?" asks the orange one. "We vacation out here to avoid the riffraff."

The yellow one slaps its head. "Oh, thank the DoGo it wasn't Jibbawk." Holding its three-fingered hands out so as to ensure it doesn't run into any obstacles, it stands and stumbles toward the growling dog.

"Mr. Killian will want to test him." The orange one remains seated. "Whether or not he survives."

Roggy leans so close that Allan can smell its rancid, dead-squirrel breath.

"Help me," Allan says. He hears his voice. He spoke! The vibration warms his throat and sends a tingling sensation into his brain. His voice isn't broken. Rubic was right. "P-please help. My uncle is hurt."

"Zip it, boy," Roggy growls. His deep voice gurgles. "It is illegal to speak until you get tested. If you don't come with us, we'll take you by force. *Everyone* gets tested."

A cold rain begins to drizzle.

Then, as if things couldn't get any worse, a dark metal object crashes through the canopy of trees and slams into the trunk of a tree. A rope, frayed and oily, is attached to the metal anchor that has been securely embedded in the tree trunk. Someone crashes through the canopy, zipping down the rope. The person hangs

on to bicycle handles that stick out of the sides of a copper box. The box has wheels in front and back that pinch the rope.

The person is a girl. Her short leather boots crunch the dried leaves when she lands on the ground. Her hair is brown and tied in a ponytail. She has a narrow face and big golden eyes. She wears a faded, blue tank top, shorts and a pack held by a single strap crossing her chest. Water cascades off her body like she has emerged from a car wash.

The surprise visitor's skin is tan, scratched and scarred. Her arms are well defined by muscles. Strapped to her thigh is a large buck knife. She quickly steps toward Allan.

Allan squeaks, "Help?"

"What is *this*?" The girl unsheathes the large, crooked knife from her thigh. "A boy? Crawling on the ground like a walrus?" she chuckles. "You need to be hung by your feet and left for Jibbawk."

The orange salamander-person says loudly, "Oh, you're always late, Asantia. But you're just in time, I think."

"He should be tested," croaks Roggy. "It is the law."

Asantia laughs. "That'll do him in. Though maybe someone will pay for him." She kneels and takes a good look at Allan. "Prat got your tongue?"

"My u-uncle. H-he's hurt."

"I came for some cake with these two cotton-candy heads, and instead, I stumble upon you. It's amazing what comes out of the waiting place," she muses. "I'm a little hard up for cash, so I'll sell you to the highest bidder. I hope you can work. If not, you'll have to be fed to Jibbawk." She touches the tip of her blade to her chin. "Now how to get you out of here."

Chapter 7
The Great Ship in the Sky

Allan panics and pushes himself back. His palms sink into the mud, and he barely moves. Asantia pulls out a rope to tie Allan's hands. He can't look away from her rope as she approaches. Anger builds in his mind. Since he can't run, he should be able to fight. He's got fists, one of which he clutches and holds up like a one-armed boxer. Too bad he was never taught to fight. He's furious that he never was. The world is so dangerous. It's only logical to teach everyone to defend themselves.

Asantia grips the rope tighter and comes at Allan. The talking dog growls. The salamander-people laugh and clap. The yellow one says, "Oh how I wish I could see this action. This is all terribly exciting. Get him!"

The orange one cries, "I hope he gets you a good bit of money. You can buy *us* tea next time."

"Leave me alone!" Allan takes a swing at Asantia. How could he have thought these *things* would help him? How could he be so stupid? These strangers are two-faced and dangerous. Rubic had warned him. Everyone has two faces. The one face people show the world and the other they see in the mirror. When that reflection is ugly, the person becomes selfish and dark with anger. Ever since Allan wound up in a wheelchair, he'd see smiles and receive phony platitudes, but then hear people talking about him behind his back. Or they'd talk about his mother or father or uncle behind his back. More and more people are proving themselves to be governed by that ugly reflection.

Asantia starts to close in but suddenly stops. She widens her stance for balance as the ground begins to shake. The ground rises and falls, almost like liquid and quickly loses its identity. Large trees topple as a roar echoes through the forest like a deep purr of a colossal dragon. The dog barks. His eyes widen like full moons, and he turns and runs.

A crack breaks the ground apart near Allan, and another crack branches off. *No!* Allan reaches out and grabs a young sapling. Its shallow roots hold Allan as the powerful earthquake ripples through everything.

The two smaller salamander-people fall off their seats and stumble away. The servant trips and falls, gets up and falls again, but is able to follow his friends.

Allan uproots the sapling he is holding as the dirt loosens and becomes soft. He's got to find something to hold onto. Allan spots Asantia's thick rope. He pulls himself to the rope and holds tight. For the moment, the anchor remains hooked to a tree.

The crack that circles the area widens, causing a huge chunk of earth to fall into the darkening crevice. The ground Asantia stands upon, falls. She jumps away and grabs the edge of the table the salamander-people were sitting at. The table's foot pedestal digs into the ground and catches Asantia. Her feet dangle into the crack, but they find a thin ledge, and she stands. She holds on to the top of the overturned table and reaches for another, more secure hold, but can't find one.

"Hey you. Help me!" yells Asantia. "You! On the box in between the handles is a little door," she says calmly. "Inside is a rope with a harness. Unroll the rope and toss the harness to me." Her eyes are wide and full of fear. Dust cakes her skin, and her previous toughness seems muted like a dull knife.

The ground stops moving, but it is impossible to tell if the earthquake is over.

Allan stiffens and feels anger electrify his nerves. "Why? You were going to s-sell me."

"I won't."

There is no way to know. Her intentions are locked in her head. Is she heartless? There was a girl in Allan's class named Tammy who always tried to cheat off his tests and bullied him on the playground. She was tall and thick. Her baby-blue eyes and blond hair gave her an innocent look, but she was nasty inside. She wouldn't steal anyone's lunch money or start fights. She would do nasty, sneaky things to you, instead, mean things that wouldn't get her into trouble. Allan remembers her giving him a hug one morning. It was a bear hug that intentionally caught his lunch bag in between them. She squeezed so hard on the lunch bag his fruit cup broke and gushed all over, and his sandwich got pulverized. At lunch, everything he had to eat looked like something someone vomited up. During a field trip, she intentionally distracted Allan and led him right into a pile of dog poop. And worst of all, when Allan would answer questions or speak up in class she would fake a sneeze or a cough so he wouldn't be heard. Thinking of Tammy makes Allan's skin crawl.

No, she is like Tammy. I'm not helping this Asantia person. Allan looks away. An aftershock rumbles the ground.

"Please!" Asantia pleads. "I just need to get to my cable. Then I can get up to my ship. I'll make you some Hantahen eggs and salt ham. Come on, boy!"

Allan looks up at the handles that are a couple of feet above him. They have two buttons on one end. One button points up, the other one down. Allan takes each handle. The wheels that pinch the rope don't move under Allan's weight. They feel solid and safe. Allan's thumb hovers over the up button.

The table shifts and the metal creaks. If it dislodges from the ground, Asantia will fall off the ledge and into the dark crack. "I'm slipping! Hurry! I won't hurt you, I promise."

What is the right thing to do? Is she wearing her other face? Is she manipulating me? Allan pushes up. Instantly, he's hoisted off the rumbling ground. He rises into the canopy and, after being whacked by a few branches, emerges from the trees into the big sky.

Asantia screams.

A large craft hovers above Allan. It resembles a blimp of some kind. Different colored fabric panels are stitched to a ribcage-like frame. Propellers extend beyond the craft, and a large pipe sticks out from the

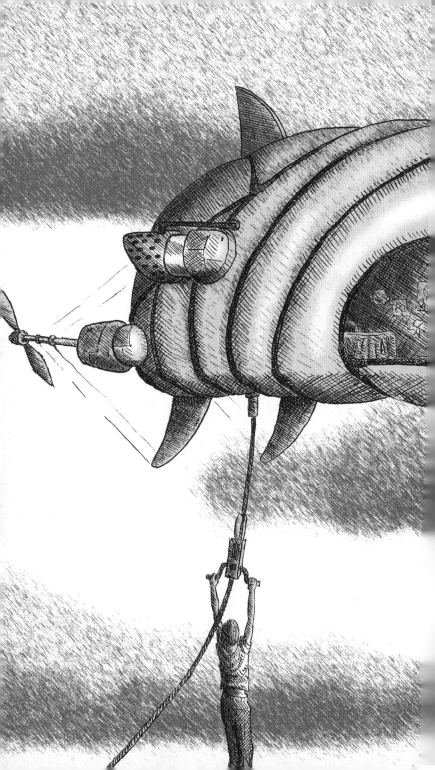

side belching black smoke. Two shark fins hang below the back of the craft and one above. The front window is long and wraps around a third of the body.

It amazes Allan, and it is stunning. But Allan can no longer ignore Asantia. She is in trouble, and no matter what she tried to do to him, he has to help. He pushes the down button.

"Thank you," She says as Allan nears the bottom of the cable. "Now throw me the harness."

Allan opens a small cubby on the copper box, unrolls the line and harness. He notices a clasp that connects the line to the box and decides on a safer course of action. He unclasps the line and reconnects it directly to the cable. He'll get her to the cable, but he's not going to stick around in case she grabs him. He tosses the harness at her and then presses the up button.

She catches the harness. "I need the handles to get up to my ship."

Allan doesn't listen. He zips to the top of the trees and stops at the door underneath the floating ship. It's got black marks and grit staining the fabric, and the metal struts are rusty but thick. There's no discernible handle or lever on the door.

Now, what? How can he get Asantia to help him without her stabbing him in the back and selling him to Mr. Killian? Or testing him? It's impossible. At any second she could overpower Allan and take him wherever she wanted him to go. He can't fly her ship. He can't even figure out how to open the door. He pounds on the metal hatch in frustration.

Just as he is about to go back down to get her,

there's movement on the horizon. Glowing balloons float toward him. Their internal lights flicker like fluorescent lights. As they get closer, Allan can see faces, strange and sad faces. Their eyes look toward the horizon, and some of their mouths are wide like they're feeding off the air itself. Below their balloon-shaped bodies are tentacles that sway in the wind.

"Come back down. I'll get you!" Asantia yells from below.

A bluish creature floats by Allan. He can see through its translucent skin. The next one bumps into the side of the airship. "Oh my," it says in a deep, slow voice.

Maybe they are friendly. The balloon-like creature floats under the ship.

"C. . . can you help me?" Allan asks.

The balloon-like creature looks at Allan. "Of course, I can. Grab hold of my tail."

This is better than helping that crass Asantia girl. Allan reaches out and grabs one of the tentacles below the balloon creature. It's soft but strong. The end of the creature's tentacle wraps around his hand then tightens like a boa constrictor.

Allan looks down at Asantia. Just before he lets go of the handles, he presses the down button, and the handles zip down the cable toward their owner. Meanwhile, the balloon creature bobs with Allan's weight but continues. There are hundreds of them in the sky, no, thousands. Some glow green, some blue.

"Okay, you can lower me down now. Somewhere safe." Allan points toward the river. "Can you go that

way? My camp is way over there." He squints, but the ground gets farther and farther away. "I think camp is that way." Allan doesn't know anymore. The floating creature looks down at Allan. Its sad eyes quiver, but it tries to smile. "I can only go one way."

It's game over for Allan. His vision blurs as tears flood his eyes. He watches his tears drip into the wind succumbing to the lure of gravity. The same gravity he feels pulling on his legs, fighting him, is not strong enough to break the grip of the tentacle.

They soar above the clouds, bathed in the purples and reds of the sunset, though there is no sun, just a swath of remaining daylight. Come to think of it; Allan can't remember the last time he'd seen the sun. It was when he was with Rubic.

Sun or no sun, wherever the balloon creature takes him, there's still a possibility there'll be a phone or a park ranger or a policeman, unless the creature has other plans. "Where are we going?"

The balloon-like creature doesn't answer. The surrounding swarm flies at the same speed and in the same direction, to somewhere just over the horizon.

"I'm thirsty," Allan whispers. He also has to pee, but he's holding it as best he can. If worse comes to worse, he'll just let it go. *Maybe the pee will rain on someone that deserves it.* That thought makes Allan chuckle.

Strange Lands

Chapter 8
The Greatest Wall There Is

The balloon-like creature flies for hours, and eventually, the night comes. The dark of deep space turns the clouds below to mere shadowy shapes, and the stars seem to flicker on. The balloon creatures appear brighter now that the daylight has completely left. They leave colored trails behind them like flags waving in the sky. Allan has never seen such beautiful color trails. Like snakes made of plasma, they trail behind then eventually fade. The balloon creatures weave in and out of formation like a coordinated dance.

Allan had seen a similar show last year during the opening ceremonies at the olympics. Fifty thousand people held up lights in a meticulously coordinated show. Their lights created images: different flags and messages of hope, triumph, and peace. It was so beautiful that his mom had made him watch it again.

Then, as a further distraction from the increasingly isolated feeling that sits heavily on his back, Allan notices a sliver of light poking up from the horizon like a nail being driven up through the clouds. It reveals itself as a sliver moon. The moon is large in the sky like a great majestic bird. It's brighter than a sliver moon should be. Midway through its ascent, another sharp sliver peeks from the horizon. Another moon! It can't be real. It has to be his imagination. Just like these balloon creatures. They can't be real either, can they? As the two moons continue to rise in tandem, a third moon appears. Allan laughs out loud. If the balloon creature hadn't been holding onto him, he'd have fallen to his death with the widest grin on his mud-splattered face.

The moons brighten the clouds below, illuminating their fluffy cotton surfaces. A lightning flash snakes through the cumulus behemoths and splits into a thousand, million branches leaving light trails in their wake. It's such a dreamy space Allan is in and is similar to the comfort he feels when falling asleep. Allan wonders if time has stopped and whether or not he'll hang from the balloon creature until the end of days.

Suddenly, the clouds break. The balloon creatures appear to be dropping, or the land is rising. A wide river snakes through a dark forest lit aglow by the three moons and trillions of stars. Beyond the river, lights dot the land. They look like stars but in a discernible pattern. *It's a city.* Far away, but it's huge. Then Allan sees a wall. It's dark and glistening. It's the largest wall Allan has ever seen. The balloon creatures all turn at the wall instead of flying over it. The wall extends as far as Allan can see and is made of large square bricks of varying shades of dark browns and grays. Moss grows on the stones and trees grow from the cracks. Vines as thick as bushes cling to the bricks. The river parallels the wall and in some places is diverted under it.

The balloon creature finally speaks, "Welcome to Lan Darr. This is as far as I'm allowed to take you." He drops Allan without warning. Allan screams as he falls until he splashes into the river. The cool fresh water washes the grime and red clay off Allan's skin. He treads water with his hands, leans back and looks up. The balloon creatures keep going to wherever they are going, and the moons smile on everything. *This is better than being captured by Asantia.* "Thanks floating things," Allan whispers.

Allan's body rudely reminds him that he needs to pee, and with no other options, he drags himself out of the water and rolls toward the wall. He smashes small twigs, bushes, and grasses. While lying on his side, he pees on a strange looking plant. It has pointy leaves, pyramid-shaped flower buds, and little purple pods on the branches. It squirms and moves like it's alive. He studies it after he zips up his fly. Did it make a squeak? The leaves are jagged and dark green at the edges. One of the pyramid buds starts to open presenting glossy purple petals. In the center of the flower is a sharp piston. The flower shudders, startling Allan.

Pain rips through his body. His fingers fumble at his neck, and he finds the sharp piston sticking out of his skin. He pinches and pulls it, but it is stuck. Again, he yanks on the piston, and it finally pulls free. As the piston releases its grip, Allan starts convulsing. He sees black, and he can't stop the spasms in his body. When the seizure ends, his entire body is numb. He turns on his side crushing more grasses and plants. His arm sinks into the mud. His mouth dries out. His throat screams in pain like he swallowed a potato chip sideways. Allan uses all his strength to roll one more time. A pale, gray, scale-covered head rises out of the mud. Sharp spikes protrude from its skull, like horns on a bull. When it sees Allan, it hisses, displaying long sharp fangs. Allan rolls again to escape, but the mud is so slick he slides into the river. Allan holds his breath as he sinks in the water. Instantly, the pain vanishes and he can move again. He pulls his arms through the water until he surfaces and rubs his neck until the pain subsides completely. His neck is swollen, but at least it doesn't hurt. Allan pulls himself to the side of the river and tries to relax, letting his head rest on his hand. He's got to be careful. "Do not stop to smell the roses in Lan Darr," he says to himself. Everything is hunting him.

He takes a sip of the river water. It's fresh and cool and doesn't have any odd flavors, so he gulps down more. He pulls himself through the water by grabbing the reeds that grow along the bank. His feet dangle, not touching the bottom. *How deep is the river?* If he's learned anything, it's that most likely there is something in the water following him. The water is dark, and it freaks him out, but he's got no other way to get around, so he keeps going. Don't think about what you can't see. *They're just shadows in your mind.*

When Allan was dangling from the balloon creature he saw that the wall surrounded a huge city, and where there's a city, there's a cop. Allan pulls himself toward the tunnel at the base of the wall where the water has been diverted. On either side of the large hole in the wall, two birds stand on pedestals that protrude from

the wall. They've got plumes of feathers on their heads and chainmail covering their chests. Their large thick beaks, blue-grey talons, and dark red feathers make them look intimidating. They're as still as statues.

As Allan gets closer to the birds, his hand snaps a twig in half. One opens its eyes and leans out from the wall. It looks back and forth. Warning signals prickle Allan's senses, so he sinks low into the water. Allan's father used to tell him, 'Our guts are sometimes smarter than our brains. Trust your gut; it'll keep you safe.' Allan didn't understand at the time, but now he does. His gut tells him that disturbing these birds would be a death sentence.

The other bird-guard wakes and, seeing his fellow guard looking around, pulls out a large bow made from a crooked branch. It nocks an arrow and readies it. Its vertical, piercing eyes see something across the river. It aims and shoots. The arrow whizzes through the air and lands in the back of a small rodent that scuttles by. The bird-guard leaps off its perch and beats its wings.

It grabs the little corpse then returns to the perch and devours the rodent with untamed snaps of its sharp beak.

When it finishes devouring the rodent, it cleans itself with a long thin tongue. The other bird-guard growls and sneers as it watches its partner groom itself. When the tension between the two ebbs, they lean back and close their eyes to the night, and all that is around.

Allan breathes, not realizing he'd been holding his breath the whole time. Shivers move through his body in waves. The night encroaches. Crickets chirp and a loon hoots in the distance. Allan can't see more than a dozen feet from the river, but he can see thick bushes and shadows, all dark and foreboding. He feels like he's being watched from the shadows, and his gut tells him to get inside the city.

Allan swims quietly under the archway. A large 'X' has been scratched into the wall. The interior of the 'X' is filled with a red liquid that catches his attention. *Isn't that the mark of Jibbawk? The dangerous thing the tea-party salamander-people were afraid of? That means it's close by and looking for food, a particular food.* Allan looks back and sees the dark forest and the river, knowing the guards are there even though he cannot see them. In the dark of the forest something lurks. Allan can feel it there. Something is watching him. Hopefully, he'll be safe in the city.

Trickling water and the raucous noise of the crickets hides the sound of his subtle movements. After the tunnel, the river splits into two directions. Tall, stone buildings border the river and block any view into the city. They are even taller than the wall. Steep stairways have been built into the sides and snake from doorway to doorway like veins feeding organs.

Allan pulls himself out of the river. There are no bushes or grasses here. Instead, there are large, rough-cut stone pieces covering all the land between the water and the buildings. He drags himself to a dark spot under the nearest stairway then pulls his feet under the stairs, so he's completely hidden in the shadow. It's too dark to go find help. He'll have to wait until daylight. Plus, that 'X' mark scared him. He can't fight Jibbawk; that's for sure. Any creature that wants him can take him.

A noise startles him. His eyes search the darkness frantically. *What is that noise?* He's never been so scared in all his life. He doesn't want to die, and he sure doesn't want some creepy creature to devour him like the bird guard devoured the rodent.

A mouse, or what looks like a mouse, forages on nearby moss. It carefully comes up to the stairway as though it can see Allan. It must have decided Allan is no threat because it grabs a hanging plant by Allan's leg, rips off a leaf and munches happily.

"Shoo," Allan hisses. The creature is small, but Allan doesn't want any odd creatures in this world near him. His instinct is right. The mouse hisses, exposing sharp fangs, and spikes pop from its fur like cactus needles. Allan freezes. The little thing looks as ferocious as a dragon. It relaxes its spikes and continues to munch on the plant. After a time, it meanders away.

Allan remains as still as possible for the rest of the night. The darkness seems to last a lifetime, and the noises in the night are strange. His eyes remain like sliced cucumbers. If he blinks, he'll miss something and wind up as a snack.

Strange Lands

Chapter 9
Fur and Frowns

Eventually, daylight comes. A clamoring of machines and a hammering in the distance jumpstart Allan's heart. Gears grind on metal, and a burnt smell lingers in the air. Humidity and warmth remind Allan of the beach. He stretches his arms and yawns. Daylight sets Allan at ease, though the day is not that bright. What's important is that the shadows have been beaten back, so if there is something out there stalking him he can see it coming.

There's a crash and someone yells, "Ah! You can't do anything right. How do you even dress yourself?" The voice sounds squawky.

Allan pokes his head out from under the stairway. A string of moss gets in his face and tickles his nose and makes him sneeze. *Did anyone hear me?* He remains still, listening to the sounds. No one comes looking, and the strange banging sounds continue. Allan rips down the moss that assaulted his nose. There's more moss and tree roots growing from every crack in the stonework. The walkway between him and the river is slick with moisture. It's not a river on this side of the wall, but a canal.

Allan's stomach rumbles, but he hasn't forgotten his mission. He needs to find someone sympathetic. Whatever kind of world the mountains hide, with all these strange creatures that speak about strange laws and strange horrors, it must contain someone with a heart. Surely someone here can look beyond Allan's apparent monetary value and lead him back to his world. Maybe they'll have some breakfast, too.

Allan peaks out from under the stairs then drags his body to the edge of the building. The river turns again, creating a new canal that heads into the city. Narrow walkways on either side are made of the same large stones, which are all damp, stained, or covered with moss or vines. The street reminds him of Venice. Further down the canal, there are stone bridges that arch over the canal.

Allan pulls himself to the edge of the canal. He wonders if jumping in the water and pulling himself along like he did in the river would be a better way to travel.

Someone's coming.

Allan quickly rolls over to the canal's edge letting his legs splash into the water. He pulls himself as tight as he can to the side hoping no one saw him. In time, he peeks. There's a tall, thin creature coming down one of the long stairways. It has dark fur and wears a raggedy leather jacket and a top hat that is bent and faded.

Two stories up is a yellow, furry thing with a short, dog-like snout and large, round eyes wearing some kind of golden headdress that shines like yellow chrome in the morning light. It yells down to the thin creature with the top hat. "It's a dreary day! A dreary day in Dantia! You won't get out of work today. No sirree. You'll finish my flooring or else I'll have you committed for re-testing. Try surviving that!"

"Yes, yes. I know how important your flooring is," mutters the thing with the top hat. "Keep up your insults and I'll set your stone crooked," it cackles. When it reaches the bottom of the stairs, it heads toward the city following the canal.

The water tickles Allan's chin as he glides through the water. He wonders about the creature in the top hat. Will it help him, some human from the so-called waiting place, or haul him to be tested or sold? He knows nothing of any of these creatures. His father used to tell him never to talk to strangers. Whose didn't? But his dad kept at it even when Allan got older. "Listen to your gut. You're riding the city bus to school now," Warren had said. "If you think someone looks mean, steer clear. Don't look at them. If they speak to you, walk to the bus driver. Terrible people are everywhere." Allan remembers rolling his eyes. "You're paranoid, Dad. I'll be fine." Now Allan tries to listen to his gut, but everything seems dangerous, mean, capable of terrible things. How's he supposed to choose who to ask for help when his gut clearly says, run, run, run from them all? Which is precisely the thing he can't do.

Allan reaches the bridge and swims under it. He finds the lip of a stone to hold himself above water. It's slimy with dark moss. A dozen four-inch tendrils with bulbs at their ends stick out of the cracks. When one touches Allan's finger they all pull back into the cracks. It startles Allan. "Is everything here creepy and slimy?"

The top hat creature Allan had been following has a boat tied to the side of the canal a few feet from the bridge. It jumps aboard, rocking the narrow, wooden boat and sending waves fleeing. The front and the back ends of the boat rise higher than the sides and are adorned with wood carvings of strange creatures. It looks too tall to pass under the bridge.

The top-hat-bird opens a box on the boat, pulls out something tan and bulging with red stuff and takes a huge bite out of it. Crumbs fly everywhere like leaping fleas, and the red stuff drips down its furry bottom lip. It takes another bite, and the drip is reinforced enough to roll off the fur and splat onto the boat. The creatures here seem slightly cultured but eat like wild animals. It bats away a dozen hungry flies.

"Arrrr. Drip in my boat. I'll clean Mrs. Filiney's favorite white dress," the top-hat-bird says almost humorously. It licks its chin with a long, bumpy tongue.

Allan eases himself back under the bridge. *Not this one. It's not a happy creature.* The top-hat-bird shrugs. "Okay flies, eat up my drips and stop bugging me." It sets the sandwich on the box then takes off its jacket exposing a bald, liver-spotted belly, then tosses his hat aside. After a short rest, it grabs a bulging bag with tools and sharp things poking from the top and leaps from the boat. It whistles a strange, high-pitched tune while heading back toward the building where Allan had first seen it.

Allan lifts himself out of the water and carefully

rolls into the boat. With some effort, he situates himself in the middle, grabs the oars, and starts to row. The boat moves away from the edge and floats into the center of the canal.

The boat rocks, but is stable. It makes Allan smile. He loves boats. He'd read about sailboats called galleons or privateers. They were huge ships with a dozen sails and deadly cannons. He read about pirates like Black Beard and Henry Morgan as they'd plundered the Caribbean ports. It was Uncle Rubic who had given him his first metal sword. Allan hadn't put the thing down for months. Only after he'd nearly impaled his grandmother's dog was the sword retired to hang on the wall.

It's a good memory and only vanishes from his mind when he hears talking. The farther he gets into town, the more creatures and people he sees. Yes, people. Actual humans. Though they're wearing strange clothing, they're less strange than the furry or feathery things.

Allan remembers Asantia and her large knife. Just because they are humans doesn't make them any less dangerous.

A small creature, as naked as a hairless cat, sits on the side of the river. It's fat, like a stumpy old man, but has only one large eye. The ugly thing picks up a long and twisted pole and casts a hook into the water. Two small fangs hang out the side of its wide mouth. The creature stares and blinks slowly as Allan passes. It only takes a moment for Allan to realize how strange his clothing must look to these people. He is dressed in jeans and an orange t-shirt with bright, sweeping designs and video game characters on the front. Until he changes his clothes, he'll be a target. So Allan stops the boat under the next bridge and puts on the jacket and worn top hat that were left in the boat. They're stained and stiff, but they'll keep him incognito. The jacket pulls on the pin-up girl Rubic pinned to his shirt. He doesn't want to lose it, so he unpins the girl and tucks her into his pocket.

Allan begins rowing again. The boat moves and, thankfully, no one pays him any attention. He relaxes while he rows, the oars moving in slow sweeping circles. The city is dense, and people are busy. Strange trees and mossy growths are everywhere. The trees have sharp leaves and spines on their trunks. *Great. Even the trees suck around here.* It also smells musty. Some buildings belch black smoke from chimney pipes, which add an acrid taste to the thick air. Another boat passes, piloted by a longhaired thing that has the face of a fox. There's lipstick on her snout lips and her eyelashes flutter.

"Watch your bow!" the fox yells, her voice high-pitched but gravelly like a witch. "Where'd you learn to steer?"

Allan stops staring and corrects his course. "Arrrr, eat my paddle," he yells in his best pirate voice. The fox-lady ignores him and continues on her way. Allan smiles at his attempt at bravado then realizes he could eat his own paddle he's so hungry. His big guts are eating his little guts, and there doesn't seem anywhere to get food. Even if his disguise helps him blend in he has no money or idea what to eat. He doubts he could get some scrambled eggs and bacon. Allan notices the half eaten sandwich on the box in the front of the boat. It looks strange. The bread is tan and covered with dark veins. The red insides might be jelly. It might be guts. Allan remembers how the guard bird tore apart the rodent like a zombie tears at fresh meat.

As he rows, he can't stop looking at the sandwich. Hunger finally wins. He steers the boat to the side and lets it bump the edge. He scoots to the sandwich and grabs it. After shutting his eyes, he crams it into his mouth.

Sweet. And the bread is crispy like a baguette. Allan hardly chews as he devours the food.

Strange Lands

Chapter 10
Killian Crow Comes

As Allan licks the jelly-like substance off his fingers, a boat slams into him. It's a much larger boat. The bow, wood ferro, the part that swoops up and out of the water, is twice as tall as Allan's boat and has a statue twice as big. The statue is of a naked woman with a cat face. Her bottom half is a mermaid, and she's framed in ornate flowers. Allan is staring at the intricacies of the carving when someone yells at him.

"Hey you!"

Allan looks toward the voice. The creature has a massive, thick beak with oily, marbled feathers. Goggles cover its eyes, and half of the beak has been patched up with a metal plate held tight by small rivets. Its wings have long thin fingers like a Pterodactyl. On the end of each finger are metal, pointy caps.

"This is my parking spot." It puts a clawed foot on the edge of the boat and leans its crane-neck way over the edge of his boat. The bird's head tips to the side as it inspects Allan. "Funny looking goat, in a stolen boat," it says. It leaps with a singular flap of its wings and lands in Allan's boat. The boat rocks then slams into the canal wall. As fast as the strike of a rattlesnake, the bird seizes Allan by the arm. It rips off the worn and bent top hat and grabs Allan's chin. It's three times Allan's size and as strong as a gorilla "A boy." it shouts.

"Please. I'm looking for. . ."

The bird pulls Allan off the bench, turns him around and grabs him by the neck. "Oh, don't you worry little boy from the Waiting Place. You're gonna make me some money." Allan struggles to slip out of the bird's grasp. It stinks and is hunted by hungry flies. "So, you want to fight me. Please! I love a good fight." The bird's grip tightens until Allan can barely breathe. Allan twists his torso and pulls at the bird's feathers. The feathers come out easily, but the bird doesn't even notice.

The bird leaps to its boat with Allan dangling like a rag doll.

"I've just the thing. . ." the bird says. It sweeps cans and trash off a filthy blanket then rips it aside. Underneath the blanket is a cage. It's rusted and bent up and looks too small for Allan, but the bird shoves him in anyway.

"Move your legs or I'll cut them off," the bird hisses like a viper. It tries to close the cage door.

"I . . .can't move my legs," Allan gasps, his neck aching.

"What's wrong with them?"

"They're broken."

The ratty-bird lifts up Allan's limp legs and shoves them into the cage. "Scrit! You won't be worth half as much." It slams its fist on the side of the boat. After a moment of silence, it concludes, "But I guess anything's better than nothing." It takes hold of the long oar that extends out the back of the boat and starts turning it in a circle. The boat pulls away from the canal's edge embracing the central current in a silent gesture. "So welcome, boy, to the rest of your life. Dantia is a great city, and as long as you can work you won't get whipped." The ratty-bird cackles.

Fish bones, what looks like rotting apple cores and mud are everywhere. It stinks.

"Excuse me?" Allan says as he tries to reason with the ratty-bird. Maybe it has a heart somewhere under its filth. Maybe he'll promise it diamonds and gold.

"Zip it, lock it up and throw away the key," the ratty-bird mumbles.

"Please, I don't know where I am. I need help. My uncle is hurt. We have gold. Lots of it." But the ratty-bird isn't listening.

As the boat floats deeper into the city, the canal widens. Tributaries split off in all directions. The buildings tower overhead and all have stairways winding around the outer walls that go up and up and up. The sun doesn't rise above the skyline because the city seems to be above the sun, above the clouds, above all that is good.

Allan wants his mother. He wants to go back in time so he can cry into her chest and be hugged. He wants someone to tell him it will be okay even if he doesn't believe them. The boat turns and enters a narrow waterway. Strangely dressed people and creatures of all shapes and sizes are everywhere, all busy. Others with long feathers and large wings fly through the air. There are shops on the first floors of the tall buildings. They have oversized doors next to large windows filled with displays. Plants and vines grow over the bricks, but there are modern elements as well. Signs stick out of the walls; crooked oil-burning lamps can be found on every corner, and a few horse-drawn carriages come and go—though the horses aren't horses at all but smaller, hairier versions.

There's a shop with huge cakes on display, a place called The Tailor and a clothing store displaying suits on mannequins. A mannequin sips on a drink from a long spiral straw leading to a ceramic mug on the floor. *So they're not mannequins showing off the latest fashions, but slaves.* The next shop is a butcher. Its window is packed edge-to-edge with skinned animals as small as mice and as large as pigs. The corpses have smeared blood on the windows. Allan looks away, fearful of vomiting the fruity sandwich he'd eaten.

The boat approaches a corner crowded with creatures and odd-looking humans. They surround a tall man standing on a box. He wears a ragged white and purple striped suit. His head is shielded by a metal pot adorned with dials and gadgets. He's in the middle of yelling at the crowd when his attention turns to the boat. The crowd complains at the man's departure, but he pushes through regardless and runs to the edge of the canal. "You there. Have you captured Jibbawk?" The man has one green eye and one orange eye and is missing two front teeth.

"Buzz off, Mister Zlack." yells the ratty-bird. "I've got another one of your kind, and he's going to Killian

Crow. He'll fetch me two hundred coins unless you're offering more?"

The man stares at Allan for a moment. "I see nothing but a speck of dust blowing through the air."

The ratty-bird elongates its neck toward the man as they slowly drift by. "Good. Then we have no problem."

"You must put your efforts into capturing Jibbawk, not some boy from the Waiting Place. Jibbawk is the real threat to all of us." The crowd behind Mr. Zlack roars in agreement. The ratty-bird laughs and turns the oar harder leaving Mr. Zlack and the crowd behind.

Allan wonders about Jibbawk. Who is it and why is everyone so afraid? Could it be more dangerous than all the other creatures? Allan imagines a huge thing with scales, bloody teeth, and big muscles. Then Allan hears loud grunts. He turns to look. The canal leads to a roundabout where a dozen elephants are drinking water through their long trunks. They are smaller than Earth elephants and have pointy heads. They chat with each other, push their neighbors playfully and take turns drinking the water.

The ratty-bird stops before entering the roundabout. A wooden dock lies to one side. The dock has three narrow slots, two of which are occupied by large, ostentatious boats with canopies, gold statues embedded in carved wood poles and red pillows. It rows slowly into the space. The ratty-bird ties a rope to an ornate gold handle, humming an out-of-tune song. It grabs the filthy blanket that is crumpled on the floor of the boat. "If you know what's good for you, you'll stay quiet, boy." The bird creature pecks at the metal cage, and as the metal plate of its beak hits the bars, sparks fly. "You a long way from home." It clicks its metal-tipped fingers together then whips the blanket over the cage.

Allan can feel the boat rock as the ratty-bird leaps out. His stomach tightens, overwhelmed by the odor of the blanket. He must do something. In just a few minutes he'll be taken to Killian Crow, whoever that is. Allan pinches the blanket and pulls it little by little until it slips off the cage. The building in front of the boat is taller than all the others. It is littered with windows, and gold figurines adorn the window sills and doorways. The ratty-bird is hoisted up the side of the building in an exterior elevator rigged with thick oily ropes, wheels, and pulleys.

"Help!" Allan yells. He rocks the cage back and forth. "Somebody. Please!" He turns and looks through the back of the cage. He sees the roundabout and the elephants. "Help me!" He screams over and over. *Someone has to help. Someone in this god-forsaken world should lift a finger for someone like me.*

An elephant looks toward him. "Yes. Come here. I need you." The elephant leans to a neighbor. Soon all the elephants are looking at Allan. Finally, one comes lumbering toward the boat. It's wearing a tall gold crown on its head, and a jewel-laden saddle sits upon its back. A few other elephants follow.

The crowned elephant reaches into the boat with its long muscular trunk and pulls the cage out. It sets the cage down between it and another elephant.

A different elephant's foot presses the top of the cage while another elephant's trunk wraps around the door and yanks it off. The Queen Elephant reaches in and pulls Allan out by the waist.

"Thank you! Now, please, get me out of here. That ratty-bird is coming back."

The Queen Elephant sets Allan on his feet, but his legs fold like puppet limbs under his weight. "He can't walk," says the elephant. "Poor boy."

"Please, I need to get home. My uncle is hurt, and he needs help. I'm not supposed to be here. I don't even know where here is."

With a momentary screech, the elevator on the side of the tall building starts back down. A gray bird with a short beak and a navy-blue top hat pokes its head out of the side of the elevator.

"Who comes?" The Queen Elephant asks.

"Crow comes. Killian Crow comes," says a different elephant.

The Queen lifts Allan off the ground then hands him off to one of her subordinates. Allan is passed, from trunk to trunk.

"You down there," yells Killian Crow. "There is a valuable fair in that boat. Guard it. Make sure it is not mistreated."

The elevator arrives, and the door opens. Killian Crow steps out casually and with grace. He wears a pressed navy suit and a bow tie. The ratty-bird follows him, chatting. Allan is set on the ground and pushed underneath one of the elephants. The ratty-bird runs to the smashed cage. "What is this?" He lifts the door. "The elephants have stolen my catch." He kicks the cage off the dock where it clatters onto his boat. "This is an outrage!"

Killian Crow turns to the Queen Elephant. "Is this true?" He eases out a short pole then whips it toward the ground. It clicks as it elongates. Killian thrusts it at the elephant. When it hits her skin, it snaps and sparks, and the elephant cries out. All the elephants start to back up toward the roundabout. Some run up the small hill in between the tall buildings. "You don't steal from me." He zaps the elephant again.

"He was freed by a band of Chicubs, sire. They came from the buildings and took him away. We tried to stop them but were unable to do so."

The ratty-bird marches up to the Queen Elephant. "She's lying! There are no sneaky Chicubs anywhere."

Killian waves his wing and the Queen moves aside. "Then let's have a look around, shall we?"

Allan is unceremoniously shoved behind a baby elephant who sits, blocking Killian Crow's view. Killian Crow and the ratty-bird push through the elephant crowd and peek behind a tree growing out of a crack in the sidewalk. They're getting closer and closer to Allan, and even though the elephants are doing their best, Killian Crow is going to find him. There is nowhere to crawl.

Chapter II
The Inventor and the Lie

Allan feels panic rising from the pit of his stomach as Killian Crow moves closer to his hiding spot. He contemplates calling out, giving himself up. It doesn't seem like the elephants can distract Killian and the ratty-bird for much longer. They're kind creatures, like the balloon creatures, but they're no match for the ruthlessness of everyone and everything around them.

Then the Queen Elephant flops her trunk in agitation. "I'm telling you, the Chicubs clambered down from the side of the building like vampire bats and took the boy. We could not move fast enough to catch them. They are fast like fleas, you know."

"Move aside." Killian orders the baby elephant. It doesn't move. Allan feels a tickle on his arm. He looks down and sees a rope that twitches. But it isn't a rope; it's a tail covered in bright orange fur. It twitches again. Horton points his trunk at the building. "Look. I see the Chicubs. They mean to get into your building and steal your gold, too."

Killian Crow turns as slow as a ticking clock and

looks up. Something is dangling from the building a few stories up. It's dark and small and upside down. It notices everyone looking at it.

"Grab on and hold tight." The baby elephant hisses. Allan grabs the tail with both hands. All the elephants make a trumpeting sound to cover the noise of Allan being dragged away at high speed.

Killian Crow raises his shock pole. It fires a bolt of electricity at the little thing hanging onto the building. The thing darts away, and the bolt hits the building, darkening the brick with burn marks. "Damn those Chicubs. They are nothing but snipping snappers. I hate them. We must kill them all!" Killian pivots to face the ratty-bird. "You have lost your fare and cost me my precious time. Leave at once or else." Killian points the shock pole at the ratty-bird but rethinks his aggression. "You will go and try to find this boy and bring him to me, do you understand?" Killian steps back toward the elevator with deliberate steps.

"Yes, I will. Bu. . . but. I will need some money to get this done. I've already spent my coin to get him here. Just a little coin or two," the ratty-bird asks, its grubby fingers clasped together over its belly. Killian ignores its plea and steps into his rickety elevator.

Allan holds the tail in a vice-like grip as he slides over the rough bricks, around and through elephant legs and over a curb of rough stone. His shirt tears under the friction. Pain stings from his ribs where the ground scrapes his skin. The tail is connected to a small creature that is driving an odd vehicle the size of a go-kart. It looks like a rat. The vehicle has large back tires and skids

on the front. Its motor belches black smoke from pipes on the back.

The creature speeds up the small hill, and when Allan hits the top, his body lifts off the grass for a moment.

He lands hard. A moan escapes his lips, and his bones vibrate like tuning forks. He is pulled under large shapes. They loom over him and resemble mushrooms. Some are taller than him, some are not, but the biggest of the big have caps as large as cars.

Through the mushroom field Allan races. His fingers weaken until he lets go of the tail. When he does, he scrapes to a stop. The tail stops, too, and the vehicle turns around. Allan looks up and sees the canopy of a large blue mushroom. Its insides are pink slots that resemble the turbine of a jet engine. Around the mushrooms are tall grasses and ball-capped bushes that look like peas on sticks. The air is even thicker, and there are bugs everywhere.

The long-tailed creature hops out of his vehicle and walks up to Allan. Its nose is long and round, and it has small rounded ears. It wears a long robe with large buttons. The creature coils its tail neatly.

"Thank you." Allan sits up on his elbows. His shirt is ripped and threadbare and his scratches sting, but they aren't bleeding too badly.

"We shouldn't stop here long, but you can rest. You're mostly safe now," It says with a voice that is nasal. "My name is Mizzi."

"Hi." Allan grabs a clump of his shirt in his hand and presses it on one of the bigger scrapes. "Why are you helping me?" He asks, grimacing in pain.

"You need it. Is there any other reason?"

Allan isn't sure he should trust this creature yet. "I'm supposed to be helping my uncle. He's hurt."

"Why are *you* helping *him*?"

"He's all I have. I . . . Guess I love him."

"It is easier for some to love than for others," Mizzi says, licking the fur on his arms and cleaning himself like a cat.

"Not too many people around here love anything but themselves or money."

"It may seem that way at first, but the longer you look, the more love you'll find." Something rustles the bushes nearby. Mizzi studies the terrain for a moment. "We should go. My home is nearby." Mizzi hands his tail to Allan then turns and runs back to his vehicle. Its engine rumbles but is surprisingly quiet for something that goes so fast.

"Ah, come on. Is there a better way for me to get around?" Allan does not like being dragged.

The mushroom in the distance topples with a crash. Something comes toward Allan.

"Hurry!"

The crashing in the bushes gets closer. Whatever it is, it's big. Allan closes his eyes. The tail finally snaps taut and yanks Allan. He slides through the path made by Mizzi. The creature zigs and zags through the mushroom stalks. Allan whacks a smaller mushroom, but it's foamy and soft. He bounces off unhurt then laughs as fear releases him. The mushrooms thin, replaced by towering trees with thick trunks and broad, dense canopies.

Mizzi parks next to a large tree trunk and leaps up like a squirrel. Allan stops at the base. At the top of the tall tree is a house made of woven grasses and twigs tucked between thick tree trunks and branches. When Mizzi gets to the tree house, he sits on a platform outside a small doorway. He wraps the part of his tail that is closest to his body around a wheel mounted to the tree trunk. "Keep holding my tail. Wrap your arm around it if you have to. Don't worry; my tail is as strong as Mythheather," he calls from above. Mizzi cranks a lever and the wheel winds up his long tail. Allan is pulled off the ground in one easy motion. The tree trunk is smooth on this side, clearly having pulled up many objects before. The higher Allan gets off the ground, the tighter his grip gets. When Allan is within reach, Mizzi grabs him by the elbow and pulls him inside.

The tree house is huge though the ceiling is low and the windows small. Allan pulls himself onto a long couch. A table is in the center of the room and is covered in metal bars, gears, and wires. A clock on the wall ticks. The kitchen is a single tub nestled inside a small counter. Candelabras line the walls and flicker light throughout the home.

Mizzi opens a cabinet made of the same interwoven grass that the walls are made of and pulls out a cup. The waterspout above the kitchen tub is a metal faucet that protrudes out of a thick tree branch. Mizzi turns the spout handle and waits. A moment later a thick substance comes out. It takes a while for the cup to fill. When it's filled, Mizzi hands it to Allan who takes the glass and smells the liquid.

"You'll love it. Tastes sweet."

Allan tentatively sips the liquid and then slurps it up. It tastes like watery maple syrup.

"I'll get you more. You just have to wait for it. Drinking from a tree teaches you patience."

Allan looks at all the stuff on the table. "Are you building something?"

"I'm an inventor."

"Your house isn't filled with inventions. Shouldn't there be little gadgets everywhere?" Allan points out the primitive candles; the tap stuck into the tree trunk and the woven grass walls.

Mizzi sits in a chair at his table. "I don't make things for myself, other than my car. I make things for others. I can't think of a better thing to do with my time."

Allan smiles and leans his head back. Finally, he's found someone who will help him. He's going to go home now. He can feel it. "Where am I anyway? I mean, I'm a long way from where I should be."

Mizzi shrugs. "Where are you from?"

"Earth," Allan replies staring at the woven grass roof.

"We are far from Earth." Mizzi laughs. "But I do know a way that will get you home."

Chapter 12
The Improbable Quest

The word 'home' reverberates inside Allan's head. He feels so far from home he'd almost forgotten it existed. He is on a mission to save his uncle's life even though he's fighting for his own. "I need to get back soon. The faster the better."

Mizzi pulls a metal bar and a screwdriver off the table and starts tinkering. "Okay then. I will help you get there as fast as I can. Though you will have to do one thing for me in return, and that one thing will be hard."

"What is it? Anything."

Mizzi speaks while he screws metal poles together, drilling holes and connecting wires. "You are from the Waiting Place, yes?" He doesn't let Allan answer. "It is where we go when we can't find ourselves. To succeed at this one thing for me, you must not be Waiting. It will be your Testing."

"Testing?" Allan's heart knocks on his chest, and he sits up. "The dog and the salamander-people at the tea party and Asantia said something about being Tested. Sounds dangerous, like it could kill me."

Mizzi shakes his head. "The Testing Games are

where some go to prove themselves. Our culture tests all young ones. It is the law. But I don't believe that there is only one way to test someone. Some young ones thrive in unbalance created by the Games. They can fix the balance. Others freeze up, and in my opinion, should be tested in other ways. Maybe they should not be proving themselves to judges but only to themselves. *You* must test yourself."

Mizzi measures the distance from Allan's ankle to his knee with a fabric ruler then goes back to the table. "Some young ones succeed rather easily. Some do not, and some give up altogether. Those that give up go to the Waiting Place where they try to forget. They're waiting for others to decide for them, or for others to be punished for things beyond our control, or maybe for just *another chance*." Mizzi looks at Allan with wide eyes. "That is you, waiting for another chance."

Allan lowers his head. "I killed my parents. If they hadn't been yelling at me for doing something stupid, they'd be alive. My dad wouldn't have been so mad and wouldn't have crashed the car." Sadness swells inside Allan like an inflating balloon.

"So when humans argue they cannot drive cars?"

"No, well, I mean. . ."

"Then you had never been yelled at while they were driving?" Mizzi probes.

"Yeah, they have yelled at me when driving before. That's not what I was . . . "

"So how can yelling have caused the crash?"

"My dad wasn't paying attention because of me."

"So no one else can cause crashes?"

Allan sighs as he realizes what Mizzi is trying to prove. "Rubic told me the other driver was on pills."

"Did you give the pills to the other driver?"

"No."

"Then I'm frankly confused. How is the crash your fault? You must remember that correlation does not imply causation."

"What does that mean?"

"It means that a connection between two things does not mean that one caused the other." Mizzi gets up and goes to a box on the counter. "Was your mother a kind woman? Would she have forgiven you for whatever made them mad?"

"She always forgave me." Allan's tears roll down his cheeks.

"Then she already has." Mizzi stares at Allan for a moment then gets up from the table. "You look a bit thin." He opens a cabinet door and pulls out a plate made of wood and a round brown object the size of a hockey puck. He sets the puck on the plate, cuts it into small pieces then fiddles with another jar. The delicious smell of sausage fills the tree house. Mizzi hands the plate to Allan. The meat pieces are drizzled with a sky-blue sauce, and a purple tomato-looking object sits to the side. "Eat. You will need your strength."

The meat is soft and salty. Its juices fill Allan's mouth and change his entire mood. "Thank you," he says with full cheeks. Suddenly he feels wide-awake, and his head stops swimming with exhaustion. He crams another bite in his mouth and savors the flavor. "This, this is so good." Allan closes his eyes as the meat triggers warmth that flows from his mouth, down his throat, and into his body. Like a balloon filling up with air, Allan feels solid again and less thin, frail and afraid. Even the "tomato" is good.

Mizzi smiles as he watches Allan eat. When Allan's mind returns from the place of tranquil nourishment, Mizzi continues. "Once you have forgiven yourself you will find the strength that waits inside you." Mizzi goes back to building some metal contraption on the table. "To get home you must go through one test. It will be difficult, but you can do it. I cannot."

"What is it? Can a cripple do something you can't? Your car moves like a speeder bike."

"If you fail you might get killed. But they have never seen a boy like you before, whereas I would be recognized and attacked immediately."

Allan stops chewing.

"Let me explain. Jibbawk needs a key that will bring it back to life."

Wait, Jibbawk is freaking everyone out. It's already here, hunting people. I've seen its mark on the bricks."

"Jibbawk's spirit is here. It's a ghost. Years ago, a young man named Ricky Boldary and Ophex warriors hunted down Jibbawk and killed him, or they thought they did. Somehow, he escaped. It didn't live long, though. Its body was found at the bottom of a thousand-foot sink hole.

"Then the murders began. It soon became clear that the spirit of Jibbawk was the killer. He was in a most unusual form. We heard from a single survivor that he was like a moving shadow and that he could change his shape at will. It has been hunting Lan Darrian's ever since.

"We now know it's looking for its body. It thinks it can be reborn, and who knows, maybe it can! The key to the tomb that houses its flesh and blood was hidden in the Lithic Fury Baroon's tooth."

"What did Jibbawk do?"

"When my father was alive, maybe fifty years ago, Jibbawk ruled all of Lan Darr. He was terrible, evil. He killed many Lupines and native Lan Darrians. Many thousands were killed over the years it was in control. Ricky Boldary was from Earth, one of the first to find Lan Darr using Hubbu pollen. My father said the Earthling was smart, a genius. He taught us to speak your language, to build factories, weapons, engines. Dantia grew and thrived for a time.

Now many live in fear. Jibbawk hunts people down, in the dark of night. Some are afraid to leave the city. They use these light stones to protect themselves, but there aren't many left. Millions live in fear, everyday. Though we are alive, most in Dantia are like you, waiting. That is why there is so much misery here. Jibbawk seeks revenge on us all for all the years it has lost. It wants to live again and believes it owns us all. Who knows what it will do if it finds its body? Jibbawk has already killed many. And it will kill again. In its body, it will be stronger. Abler."

"What am I supposed to do?"

"Retrieve the key for me."

"Why not leave the key where it is? It's been hidden all this time."

"I've gotten word that Jibbawk has killed Mayor Mortimer. We believe the mayor has surrendered the location of the key. I, and many others, have been trying to find a way through the Lithic Furies, but cannot. They are taller and more protective than ever. They won't recognize you, but they'll attack anyone from Lan Darr."

"What will you do with the key?"

"The key will let me open Jibbawk's tomb. I need the key because there is no other way to open the tomb. I've tried. So, with the tomb open, I will wait for Jibbawk to come and reenter its body. Only then can I banish the evil creature to a land ten thousand years away."

"Okay. But one more question. How do you expect a cripple to do this?" Allan finishes the meat and licks the plate clean.

"With this." Allan looks up. Mizzi holds up a contraption that looks somewhat like a wind chime entwined with the guts of a computer.

Mizzi kneels next to Allan and starts fitting the contraption to his legs. "I just have to get this right." Mizzi straps a thick leather belt around Allan's waist and cinches it tight. The buckle is a metal box with small dials and a glass screen. The belt is connected to shock-absorbing leg pieces. There are straps at the thigh, calf, ankle and foot. Each one is cinched as tight as they can go. Allan's borrowed jacket and his jeans bunch under the pressure. Mizzi connects wires to the shocks and tests them with a gauge. The needle jumps, which Allan guesses is good.

Mizzi retrieves a box from the table and opens

it. Blue light bursts from the box. Inside is a rough, asymmetric, clear stone that shines from its interior and spins in a million different ways. "This will power your new legs." He puts the stone inside the waist buckle then screws the buckle closed.

"My new legs?" Allan's voice quivers. He sits up and touches the metal, afraid he'll break them.

"Yes, but these are temporary. I'm sorry they can't be permanent. The power will last for only six hours. Then the legs will be useless. You must go to the Lithic Fury Baroon and steal his bottom tooth. And you must go now as the day sets."

Mizzi hands Allan a hand drawn map. It has a sketch of what the Lithic Fury Baroon will look like and how to get to it. Mizzi loops a long rope over Allan's head and under one arm. "You can do this. Success will set you free."

"I hope so."

"Don't just hope. Make it so."

Mizzi lowers Allan from the tree house with his tail and sets him on his feet. The mechanical legs hold Allan up. He's standing! It has been so long since he has stood without someone holding on to him. He looks around, savoring the view, not wanting it to end. It's good to be tall, and then he realizes, even though he had to buy new pants a month ago, that he has grown taller. By maybe three inches. Maybe more.

Mizzi hollers from the tree house, "The back of the belt reads the signals from your spine. It will tell the legs how to work. All you have to do is walk."

Allan thinks about moving. His legs won't budge.

"Move, now," he tells them. Still, they don't move. He wonders about Mizzi's plan and about his ability to use the legs efficiently. Maybe his brain had forgotten how to walk. He recalls that sometimes at night he could feel his legs. It was what the doctors called a 'phantom leg.' He wasn't feeling the actual nerves in his legs, but the sensations that his brain remembers. So somewhere in his skull, he knows how to walk.

"Heads up," Mizzi calls out.

Allan looks up as a large pan falls from the treehouse. It drops quickly toward Allan's head. At the last second, Allan leaps away. They worked! When he lands, he wobbles like a marionette but doesn't fall. This time, when he orders his legs to move, they do. He takes a step, and it's more stable. The next step after that is fluid, natural. He's walking again. Allan spins, his arms stretch outward. It feels so great. He hops over a small bush and then does a little dance. Oil leaks from the shocks, but not much.

"Okay, now you must hurry," Mizzi says from above. "Though it is good to see you dance."

"I got this." Allan runs through the thick mushroom forest. He's breathing hard but not because his muscles are doing any work. The mechanical legs do all the work. The exhilaration Allan feels is similar to the moment a roller coaster races down the track. He smacks a soft mushroom cap as he passes it and laughs.

When Allan gets to the edge of the forest, he stops. In front of him is a wasteland. To the horizon are towers of rock, dead trees and broken buildings, miles, and miles of desolation. But from Mizzi's explanation, the

towers of rock are not dead at all. They are the Lithic Furies, creatures that live in the rocks. They have been sculpted by erosion and time and born out of the rubble of a ruined city. They have grown taller and taller over the years and have become powerful. They don't let anyone roam the ruins, no one.

At least, no one from Lan Darr. Allan was instructed to move quickly before the Lithic Furies realize he's a threat.

"Good thing about rocks," Mizzi had said when they were back at the tree house. "They think slowly. It'll take them a while to recognize you as a threat, and once they do, you'd better be gone."

Allan tells his legs to move like a cheetah, and they do. The first Lithic Fury he passes towers over his head. Its rock body is thin and compiled of archways and square bricks. At the top is a cluster of stones that resemble pincers or sharp beaks. The rock tower bends its neck down to look at Allan but doesn't react. Allan continues right into the heart of the rock formations. Some have long necks, small heads with sharp teeth in their mouths and arms set in logical places, but most aren't recognizable as creatures at all. They're simply thin towers built from the ruins that once littered the dusty ground.

Allan inspects the drawing of Lithic Fury Baroon then searches the rock towers. A dozen heads turn and look at him. The shadows in the failing light are dark. Dust blows and dry thorny weeds tumble around. "Nothing lives there, except the rocks," Mizzi had told him.

Allan sees a cluster of small rock formations looking at him. Were they baby Lithic Furies? *Mizzi said the rocks were dangerous, but how fast can a rock monster really be?* For a brief moment, he thinks he's not in any real danger, and that Mizzi must be a scaredy-cat. Then one of the rock towers cracks shedding dust and small stones as it twists toward him. A thousand pounds of rock comes crashing down. Allan's mechanical legs launch him three times as far as any average kid could jump. The rocks tumble to the ground then pick themselves up. Allan will be crushed like an egg stomped under a boot if the boulders or bricks fall on him.

Finally, he sees the Lithic Fury Baroon. It's one of the larger stone beasts in the middle of all the others. Allan sprints toward it. They're all watching and thinking about this strange boy and his squeaky, oil-leaking leg armature. There's no way to climb Baroon. Its neck is too thin and uneven. Then Allan sees another way.

He leaps onto a smaller stone arch that is shaped like the backbone of a dinosaur and runs up. There's an arm that arches over to a nearby rock monster. Allan jumps to the arm and scuttles up it. His arms wobble back and forth, balancing him. When he gets to the end, he stops. There's a large gap between it and the other rocks. The rock moves. Allan jumps just as the head of the other rock swoops by, nearly decapitating him. Allan lands on a rock that sticks out of the neck then climbs the neck using the protruding stones like a ladder.

Baroon is next to him now. Allan slips the rope off his arm and ties one end into a loop. The rocks all around him shift and rumble. He's about out of time, but how does he open Baroon's mouth?

"Hey, Baroon. Come get me." Allan yells.

The Lithic Fury Baroon turns its massive head to the side and considers Allan. It opens its long, wide mouth and thrusts toward Allan. Allan waits for only a moment. The mouth comes at him, fast. He's only got a second, only one chance to do this right. *No hesitation.* Allan whirls the looped end of the rope like a lasso, holding onto the other end tightly.

The loop lands perfectly around the Baroon's tooth. Just before Allan is snapped up, he jumps. The rope tightens, which cinches the loop tight around the tooth. Allan swings through the air. The Baroon turns just as its tooth snaps off. Allan falls, but his metal legs absorb the weight when he lands on his feet. He tugs on the rope and pulls the tooth toward him. He snatches the heavy stone tooth off the dusty ground and holds it tight to his chest. There is an impression inside the rock-tooth that holds the key. The key is rusty and old, has long crooked teeth and has the letter 'J' cut out of the round handle.

Allan pockets the key as the stones all around him start to move. The sand under his feet rises. He's hoisted in the air on a large arching stone. Allan slides down. When he lands on the dirt, he runs. Rocks fall all around him. One hits his shoulder, knocking him down. Dust clouds his vision and makes him choke, but he runs faster. He sees sparks, shooting like miniature fireworks, popping from the gears of his mechanical knees.

He finally reaches the end of the dusty field of

rocks. The hundreds of Lithic Furies should be chasing him. They might be slow to think, but they were quick in their attack. However, none of the towering rock creatures pursue Allan. They must know they cannot keep up with him, so they stand and stare, defeated. The rock towers collapse one brick at a time. *They've given up. Are they dying? Can a rock thing ever really die? Do they feel the defeat? Were they around before keeping the key or created solely to be guards?* As the cloud of dust gets larger and comes toward Allan, he turns and runs. Allan feels a twinge of guilt and sadness.

Is it worth it? If Mizzi's plan works, Jibbawk will be gone for good. A lot of people will be saved. It has to be worth it. The survivors that live in Lan Darr will surely think so.

All, Allan, has to do now is get the key to Mizzi, and then he can go home. He runs for the pure pleasure of the wind in his face, which spreads joy throughout his body. He circles the Lithic Fury territory and heads back toward the mushroom forest, hoping he is moving in the right direction. There are more ruins out here, remnants of a much smaller town. The trees are crispy and burnt, and the stones are black marked and crumbling. A fire tore through here a long time ago.

Allan turns onto a street. His elation implodes in his chest like the popping of a balloon. There, in between more ruins, stands a creature with a large sharp beak. It has thin arms with pincers at the ends instead of hands. Allan recognizes it. It's Jibbawk! *It looks just like Rubic described. How is this possible? How did Rubic know?*

Jibbawk comes at Allan, but Allan is frozen in fear.

He's not sure if what he's seeing is real. But it is real. It is the feared Jibbawk. There's one difference from Rubic's description. It doesn't have quills like a clown fish. Something else covers its body, something that moves. Bugs. Jibbawk is covered with thousands of large black bugs.

Chapter 13
Beetles that Became One

Allan can't move or even think. In the fading light he sees not a huge bloody monster or a dagger-toothed beast adorned with muscles, but a thin figure that is already dead and just as terrifying. It has made an entire city cower in fear because of its ruthlessness. It will derive pleasure from killing Allan.

Jibbawk waves at him, taunting him, as it moves forward. Allan tries to step back, but he can't. Bugs fall off Jibbawk as it moves. They crawl to catch up with it. As Jibbawk approaches, Allan realizes Jibbawk isn't dark because of the growing night. It is pitch black because the bugs are beetles as dark as black holes. It has red glowing eyes that emanate a heat from within them like a volcano ready to blow.

"I will have the key whether you give it to me, or I take it from your dead fingersss," Jibbawk says, reaching out for Allan. Its voice is hoarse but steady. It feeds off Allan's fear, breathing it in like pure oxygen. "Sss, I only want what I deserve," it says. "When everything is taken from you by forccccce, is revenge, not the only way to be whole again?"

It's hard to picture this thing, this moving, churning, angry apparition as something alive, a ruler. It must have looked very different. What did its body look like?

Jibbawk reads Allan's resistance and gives up its sympathetic appeal. "I made thisss, all of thisss, possible. Everyone owes me their lives. They should all be on their knees at my feet. And ssso should you!"

Its patriarchal plea falls on deaf ears. The shepherd that'll kill the sheep to keep them in line is no shepherd at all. It doesn't look so smart to Allan, just ruthless and desperate.

Jibbawk lunges. Allan's brain snaps into focus. He sprints in between two buildings and turns down a parallel street. He runs through another gap between buildings. Shadows from dead trees startle him. He gasps as he searches for a way through the thickets and the thorns and the boulders and bricks.

Every building is in ruins, but some walls are more intact than others. He looks over his shoulder. Jibbawk isn't far behind. It is truly the most frightening creature in this entire world.

It doesn't look like Jibbawk is running because the beetles that form its legs are shifting and rotating, moving like little wheels. To move faster, Jibbawk bends down and lets its entire lower half break apart. Now the beetles roll Jibbawk along like it's on a tank track. It makes a sickening clicking, snapping sound.

Allan's belt beeps. He looks at the light where the battery crystal is. He's used about half the power. He's got three and a half hours before the legs are useless. So Allan runs harder. Fear courses through him in waves.

He runs through another alley then down the street and rests against a pile of large bricks. It's dark now. Jibbawk is nowhere to be seen. Allan can't run forever. He needs a plan, some way to hide or to fight. But how can he fight a ghost made of beetles?

There's a building that still has a roof and four walls so Allan ducks inside.

He immediately regrets his move. Hiding isn't a good plan. If he's found, he will be trapped. There's no window, no hole in the wall and only one way in or out. A dry twig snaps just outside. Oh, no! Should he run? Should he stay? He needs to make a quick choice again and he can't. He's frozen with indecision. Allan makes for the doorway, but Jibbawk steps into it. Allan scampers back to the far corner wanting to scream, wanting to fight, but able to do neither. Jibbawk takes one claw and scratches a large 'X' on the wall. The 'X' bleeds red. It places its pincers on either side of the doorway; beetles break off and crawl along the walls. They disengage from its feet as well. Jibbawk melts into the walls and floor as thousands of beetles come closer and closer. Their pincers snap, snap, snapping.

"That key is mine!" Jibbawk roars. "And ssso is your sssoul."

Anderson Atlas

Chapter 14
Rubic and the Dawn of Night

Rubic lies half a galaxy away, still under the large boulder on the riverbank. Night has fallen, and an owl stares at Rubic in wonder. A curious raccoon scuttles up to Rubic and sniffs his cheek. Its whiskers tickle Rubic's skin, and he wakes with a start. The raccoon sprints away, but the owl stays and watches. Rubic shivers. He's confused, but for only a moment. Panic sparks his consciousness awake. "Allan! Allan!" He tries to move, but can't. His entire right side is numb. A huge rock holds him in the mud; his arm lost underneath the stone's massive weight. He twists his legs back and tries to push the boulder off. *How long have I been here?* The stars above him number in the millions and the moon is big and bright. There's a rustle in the trees. This is bear country, and he's as vulnerable as a shish kebab at a dinner party. "Allan?" he says hoping the sound is his nephew. There's no answer.

Rubic feels around under his body and starts digging out dirt and stones. The boulder starts to lean on him more. Pain destroys his thoughts in one fell swoop. He cries out to help relieve the pressure of pain in his brain. After a minute the pain settles. He notices a small rock dam that is diverting the water around him. Keeping the water off him has kept him alive. Allan must have built it.

"Allan! Where are you?" The only reply is from the crickets. "Crap, kid. You must be trying to get help. How are you gonna get anywhere without your chair?"

Rubic grabs one of the larger stones from the dam, being careful not to dismantle the dam completely. Moving carefully but quickly, Rubic props the rock on one side of his arm then grabs a similar sized rock and wedges it on the other side. He starts to dig under his arm again, one scoop at a time. After several scoops, the heavy boulder starts to fall again but is held up by the rocks. He keeps digging until his arm moves. He yanks his arm out and rolls away. The two rocks give out, and the boulder falls. The boulder splashes into the river in a surprisingly subtle motion.

Much worse than before, pain shoots up Rubic's arm. His fingers are black, and he has a gash running up his forearm all the way to his elbow. It's perforated and bleeding heavily now that the stone isn't pinching the wound shut. Rubic unclips his paracord bracelet off his wrist. The bracelet is a braided military strength rope. From a pocket of his fishing vest, he pulls out a pocket knife and cuts the end of the braid. It untangles easily and then he lays it across his lap. He cuts one entire lower pant leg off and uses it to wrap his arm. He then ties the paracord around his forearm using hand and teeth.

"Where did you go, Allan?" Rubic looks around.

The shadowy forest watches him. Shivers echo throughout his muscles. He pulls his cell phone out of one of his many vest pockets, but it's been damaged by water. He throws it in a tantrum.

"Allan!" he calls out. The pain in his arm makes his teeth hurt. He can wiggle his pinky which is good. The circulation needs to return fully. If it doesn't, the doctors will have to amputate his arm. The pain is too intense, and he can't hold his hand up. So Rubic takes the remaining paracord and fashions a sling that goes over his head and around his wrist to hold his arm up. His hand immediately feels better. He breathes the cool night air while ordering himself to relax.

Rubic gets up and sloshes across the moonlit river and heads back up the river toward camp calling for Allan. Rubic strains his eyes hoping to see tracks, but the ground is dark. He thinks he can see drag marks on the edge of the forest. But following it leads nowhere. If someone had to drag themselves through the forest they'd have to find the path of least resistance. Rubic tries to find this path, but can't. Now he's deep in the forest and it's too dark to see anything. Instincts tell him to walk parallel with the river. He hikes around a huge boulder and over fallen logs and up a steep incline. All the while he keeps the trickling sound of water within earshot and wonders how Allan would be able to drag himself through the ferns and over the sharp rocks and pine needles.

When Rubic gets to camp, he sees his truck. It was pushed off the hill he'd parked on. Now it lies on its side, smashed against a large tree. He kicks the hood.

The ranger station is at least eight miles down the road. Are there other campers who haven't been swallowed up by the freak flood? Rubic likes this place because of how secluded it is, how quiet it is, and how far from the loudmouths and the mundane tasks of modern-day life it is. Now he wishes there were a few other loudmouths around to help him.

Rubic finds his cooler half-buried under mud and flips it open. The ice is still in cubes. He stuffs his mouth full of the lunch meat he brought and chugs some water. He unzips his first aid kit and pops four ibuprofen. His body feels as heavy as lead, so he sits. Bending down sends pain out of his ribs and arm. Even in the blue moonlight, he can see that his entire arm is purple and bruised. He takes some ice from the cooler and massages his arm. He calls for Allan, but only hears his voice echo off the nearby canyon walls and not a peep more. There should be frogs burping or crickets chirping, but there's only a stony silence. There is no tent, no wheelchair, no firewood, no stove. Everything has been washed away.

Rubic starts hiking down the dirt road. The moonlight illuminates the road, making it appear plastic. It's helpful because dark swaths of forest surround everything else. Eight miles downhill should only take three hours.

An hour later he sees lights approaching. He waves his good arm in the air and hollers. The truck pulls to the side of the road. It's white with a blue stripe down the side and has the postal insignia on its door. In the back is a large bag full of boxes and letters. Rubic runs up to the driver's door. "Hey! I need help. Me and my nephew were hit by a flash flood. I've been pinned under a boulder and knocked out. I woke up, and he's nowhere."

"Oh never a dull moment up here," the postman says. "I was wondering where all the water damage has come from. I see it all the way down the mountain. A swath of water took out an acre of bushes. It's crazy. C'mon, hop on in."

Rubic runs around to the passenger side. "Thank you."

"I'm Larry. I'm the mailman. You're lucky I'm so late. Normally, I'd be at home watching the game on TV. Not too many people come up to this part of the mountain."

"I don't feel lucky," Rubic says.

Larry gets on his walkie-talkie and calls the Ranger station. He turns to Rubic. "Help's a-comin'."

"Thank you." Rubic sways. "I'm about ready to pass out. For once I'm thanking the postal service, not cursing it." Rubic looks out the back window, expecting to see walrus creatures poking up from the potholes, but they aren't there. He sighs.

"More mail every year. Someone's got a mighty fine business up here, I guess. Plus, I deliver the mail to the residents that live up there past the glacier. It's a year-round hazard. I've got to fight walruses to get to their igloos." Larry laughs. "Just kidding. But y'know, this narrow canyon is the main flood zone for the lake. I've never seen it, but folks say that every so often a large chunk of that glacier breaks off and falls into the lake. Yup. The lake overflows the dam and floods the valley. This one must have been a big break. Never seen anything like it," Larry says, making chitchat.

Rubic is too worried, in too much pain and too anxious to listen to Larry. "Look, my nephew's lost up here. We both were swept away. I just woke up. I've been out all day. My arm is…" Rubic shows him his purple, blood-splattered arm.

Larry clicks on the cabin light. "Good Lord. You need a doctor."

"Only after we find my nephew."

"If he tried to go get help, he could have gone a long way in eight hours. Yup."

"I don't think so."

"Why's that?"

"He's paralyzed, and his wheelchair was washed away."

"Oh dear. I'm sorry, I'm going on and on. This is terrible. Let's get to finding your nephew." Larry hits the gas and drives toward the campsite. "We can have a search party out here lickety-split."

Chapter 15
Cornered

Allan watches thousands of pincher beetles skitter towards him. Their shells are shiny and sleek, and their antennas search, feel for Allan. Jibbawk moves into the room like a mudslide. Only its body, face, and eyes remain in their shape. Those hideous red eyes glow hot and are slit vertically like a cat's. Allan can't watch anymore. He closes his eyes, but he can hear the beetles come for him like the clicking of tumbling glass marbles. The ceiling of the house cracks. Dust rains down. As the crack widens, large chunks of ceiling break open and lift away. The night sky is in full bloom. Three moons stare down at him. Something leans over the hole in the roof. It's a Lithic Fury!

This is it. Game over. He won't get another chance. He braces himself and says over and over, "Please, no. I don't want to die..."

Rocks pinch Allan around the waist and lift him up and out of the room. The air is squeezed out of his chest.

Allan is gently set upon a rock that protrudes from the Lithic Fury's neck. The ground is thirty feet below.

Allan looks down to see Jibbawk and his legion of bugs break for the doorway, but not before the Lithic Fury topples the rest of the house on Jibbawk and his beetle crew.

Allan considers leaping off the Lithic Fury and running away. His mechanical legs should handle the jump.

"You don't have to go," says the Lithic Fury. Allan doesn't hear the voice with his ears. He hears the Lithic Fury's voice inside his head. "I won't hurt you," it says.

"But I stole the key from the Baroon's mouth. You were all sworn to protect it. Don't you want it back?" Allan says.

"We have guarded the key for a long time. But Jibbawk is still around. Even under the rocks, it is not gone. It is the spirit of its elder self. Alas, we see now that while we kept Jibbawk from its body, it was not defeated. We hope you have a better solution."

"Mizzi does. He wants to set a trap for Jibbawk. Get its body and its ghost together again then confine them both forever. He says he has the power to do that now."

"Goooood." The Lithic Fury's voice vibrates Allan's ribs like they are tuning forks.

"I thought you were all dead," Allan says as he and the Lithic Fury head down a road through the ruins of homes and buildings. The Lithic Fury stomps along, shaking the ground with each step. It moves slowly but covers a lot of ground with long strides. In time the Lithic Fury gets to the end of the charred ruins.

"We did lose our purpose. So, we started to fall

apart. It is hard because we cannot do the thing we were meant to do. But we don't want to fade away. The only choice we have is to find another purpose. We can remake ourselves into anything we wish."

Allan looks at his legs, feeling the Lithic Fury's words reverberate throughout his mind and echo in his chest. "I have to do the same."

The two travel through the countryside of Lan Darr toward the city of Dantia and toward Mizzi's tree house that lies in the heart of the mushroom forest. It is dark, but lights on the horizon guide the way.

"I don't recognize this area. Are we going the way I came?" Allan asks.

"This is the fastest way to the mushroom forest."

At the top of a grassy hill is a crowd of people. They are cheering next to a pathway of hot coals. The area is lit up with bright torches. The Lithic Fury steps away from the crowd. "They will fear me. I do not want to disturb the Testing."

Allan looks more closely. "That is the Testing?" The children and young creatures being tested are wearing toga-like robes lined with golden patterns and intricate symbols. Though the horses are walking on the coals, they don't seem to be bothered by them. They are thin and bony, and their hooves are a foot tall and as solid as stone. Not a horse, but more of a nightmare version of one.

"The Shadic ruler, Jibbawk, started the Tests as a way for slaves to gain freedom. Only the worthy could escape from a life of service. All Shadic empires used some form of a trial like these. They test strength, balance, will power, patience and intelligence. However, they are tricky and can be brutal.

"But Jibbawk doesn't rule anymore? Why are the Testing still going on?" Allan wonders.

"Men's hearts are hard to change. Many still see value in the Testing. There is still slavery as well. There are many aspects of Shadic rule that are still used."

"That sucks." Allan watches the commotion of the crowd. "What is this test?"

"They balance on a horse and race each other over coals." The Lithic Fury says. "This is the first and most benign test the children will go through."

The crowd surrounding the finish line waves torches and whoops and hollers, but the kids are still and focused.

Allan watches them as they pass. "I never thought what they're doing was possible."

The Lithic Fury answers, "There are five tests in total. Some die in the games; some remain enslaved, and some are set free."

One contestant falls off his horse and into the hot coals. His robe catches fire, and he leaps up and runs into armed guards. They snatch the boy, put the fire out and haul him away. Allan notices that the boy's sleeve is pinned to the shoulder fabric. The boy has no arm. "Why are they, slaves?"

"We are all slaves in some way," The Lithic Fury answers. "I was a slave to protecting the key for decades. Some are slaves to their work and some are slaves to their fears. . . And there are some that still tie themselves up to the ghosts of their forefathers."

"I don't have any choice, and that makes me feel like a slave. I have to go to school. I have to do chores. Now I'm still a slave to that stuff and also to my wheelchair."

The crowd starts chanting. There are only two more balancers left on the course. The horse behind the leader leaps into a gallop. The boy remains on its back. It startles the lead rider, and he falls into the coals. The boy gets to the finish line and is lifted off the horse by the crowd. Some cheer, others boo, and the fallen boy is carried off.

Someone notices the Lithic Fury.

A man pulls off his top hat exposing wild frizzy hair. He points and yells. The crowd turns. Everyone flees in terror.

"We must go now," the Lithic Fury says as he starts to move quickly into the Mushroom forest. "I do not want them to fear me."

"You know, it's weird. I sometimes get the feeling people fear me, too," Allan says. "Not because I could hurt them, but it's like they don't know what to say around me." He leans against the rough stone of the Lithic Fury's long neck and rests his head.

After a dozen long and careful steps, they arrive at Mizzi's tree. It lifts a rocky arm up to the window and lets Allan crawl into it. "Goodbye, Allan."

"Thank you. . .What should I call you?"

"I'm Bink. At your service." Bink moves off and Allan worries what it will do. What will it be good at? What will any of them do now that they have no chains holding them down?

Inside Mizzi's home, there's a note on the

table. 'Allan, I've begun preparations for Jibbawk's confinement. I couldn't wait for you. Follow the map and meet me at the Field of Marrow next to the Tower of Stepps and the Lichen Lake. I've drawn a map on the back of the note. Be careful. You must not fail.'

Strange Lands

Chapter 16
Time Won't Last

Allan looks at his legs. He has less than two hours of battery life remaining. Time. All he feels is the passing of time. Time is his constant companion, and like a parasite, it feeds off his beating heart.

Allan looks at the ground below Mizzi's door. It's far, but not for his mechanical legs. Allan leaps from the tree and lands on his feet. He runs through the mushroom forest, leaving a trail of oil drips behind.

Deep shadows are everywhere, and Allan can't see very well. If not for the three moons, he'd be blind. Fireflies leap away when Allan pushes through the bushes; butts burn bright then fade like dying sparks. Allan tries to retrace his steps to the city by following the obvious drag marks. The path dredged by Allan when Mizzi pulled him to safety flattened and uprooted tons of baby mushrooms and small plants. It's only when Allan comes to a couple of different trails that he gets confused.

Allan tries to read Mizzi's map, but it isn't as accurate as it needs it to be. Mizzi designated the mushroom forest by drawing squiggly lines, and the line to the city is an arrow. But which way is the arrow pointing?

"Come on, Mizzi. Ever thought of inventing a compass?" Allan says, frustrated and tired of being alone in the dark. He knows, just knows, that something is going to jump out of the shadows and eat him alive.

As Allan continues, the forest becomes increasingly dense, forcing Allan to zigzag around stalks that tower over him and thick, spike-covered bushes. There are more bugs now. Allan smacks them away as they incessantly nag his face and eyes.

He walks for a long time.

A beep alerts him to the belt. The mechanical legs have an hour left. Allan starts to jog. Panic sits underneath his skin like lava in a fissure. If he starts to panic, he'll shut down. What did his dad used to say? "I count." Warren had said at Allan's first swim competition. "You swim hard, and you swim fast. Exercise engages the mind in something other than the cycle of fear. Your brain likes to focus on your movement. It drowns out everything else." Allan's dad was so smart. At that swim meet, Allan had won his first trophy.

Allan moves faster. His pulse rises and his breathing increases. He pushes through tall furry bushes and past fallen branches that are covered in scales. Faster, he moves. Soon, his mind isn't focusing on anything but movement.

Allan reaches Dantia's tall and forbidding outer wall. It is still a welcome site. He forces himself to catch his breath so he can creep to the river, expecting guards. There are none.

The water is as still as glass and reflects the moon

and starlight with perfection. There are flowers on either side that he'd not noticed before. They are deep purples and light blues. Some are round and large, and some are soft and small. Some lean toward the moons and the others are heart-shaped buds. They might be the same shooting buds Allan ran across when the balloon creatures dropped him in the river. He'll stay clear of them. He's getting the hang of traveling through dangerous places.

The stars above pack the sky. There are so many other solar systems out there. *Is Earth up there? Did the balloon creatures travel through some kind of wormhole? Maybe.* The chill of the air prompts him to cross his arms. It's beautiful here, but a long way from home.

Allan follows the water and thinks about Rubic. Is he alive? If the cruelty of fate comes bashing through his life again, then his uncle will be dead. He'll have only his grandmother and some cousins left, but he doesn't know them very well.

The river is diverted under the wall in places, but not here. Here the wall and the river do not intersect. The mechanical legs beep. Thirty minutes left on the clock. In desperation, Allan swims across the river to the wall. He searches the stone. There are gaps at every brick and long trailing vines that might hold his weight. Allan starts to climb. His shoes fit into the small cracks, and the vines are indeed thick and sturdy. He climbs and climbs and climbs. As he nears the top, he looks down. Dizziness overwhelms him and forces him to squeeze his eyes shut. He's so high up. Too high up and with no way to turn back, he continues.

At the top Allan reaches for the top of the wall. He can't quite reach the last stone. Allan reaches again. No good. He's too short.

Allan bends his knees, his feet crammed in a gap in the stones, and he's holding tight to a vine. He leaps, trying to jump to the top of the wall. The mechanical legs overpower his jump, and he goes over the top. Allan panics and tries to turn, but can't. He falls feet first into the darkness below.

His feet touch down easily in a soft mound of moss, and his hand lands on the ground, keeping him from falling forward. The moss is as cushy as a foam mattress. Allan rolls back on his butt and laughs. Clearly, he has nine lives.

Now inside the wall, the brightness of Dantia's lanterns welcomes him. Allan stands and brushes off mud and clumps of moss. Movement catches his eyes. It's a dog standing across the canal. It has long matted fur and long ears that point straight up like a rabbit's ears. The dog's head turns to the side in a curious manner, and then it barks.

Behind the dog is a tall building with lots of windows and doors and stairways leading to other levels. The dog spins in circles while barking ferociously and flinging foam from its jowls. Torches are lit, and lights flip on. People come to their windows and yell and point.

Everyone has heard of the Boy from the Waiting Place, and now the alarms have been triggered. Allan turns to the left. The canal makes a hard right and heads into the city. At the turn, a building has been built

against the wall. People and strange-looking creatures come out of the ground level door. To the right is another building, and the dog is across the canal in front of him. He has nowhere to run to. From the left comes a boat. It has a motor of some kind. A spotlight turns on him. A garbled voice, projected from a crude cone, orders him to stay where he is. The last thing he needs is to be taken into custody. But even if he had a direction to run, his legs are going to give out at any minute. He might as well give up. Maybe Mizzi can bail him out of jail. But will they take him to jail? He might be sold, tried like a criminal, or beaten. They'll take the key from him and who knows what else. He can't give up. There has to be somewhere to go.

A snail, the size of a baseball, crawls up the side of the wall. Its body glows from bioluminescence. The shell is thick and spiral and black with white stripes. The snail's slimy body and sticky optical tentacles turn to Allan. Then it shrieks and snaps its head into its shell. It falls off the wall and rolls into the canal with a splash. Allan jumps into the water, grabs the glowing snail and swims down as hard as he can. He used to be a fast swimmer, the best in his age group. His brain awakens that dormant part of his brain, and powers through the water. He coordinates his arms and legs, maximizing his speed like it was only yesterday he was competing at the Local Swimming Committee. Chills erupt from his skin.

The snail lights Allan's way in the dark water. He sees pipes leading in every direction. The streets and buildings aren't built on solid ground but on dark, algae-covered columns. The water flows in many directions, all of which are bad options.

Something spears into the water. It looks like an arrow but has hooks on the back of the point. If it hits Allan, he will be pulled out of the water like a fish. Allan grabs onto a pipe to keep himself still. He can't breathe, but he can't surface. They'll get him. His lungs pull on his mouth and throat as they try to force him to breathe.

He looks at the pipe and sees a small bubble rise from a seam in the pipe. A bubble! Allan pulls on the pipe then kicks it. The seam widens. Large bubbles rise to the surface. Allan puts his head into a bubble and sucks it in. It's air. He expected it to be stinky or even gassy, but it's just air.

He takes a deep breath and follows the pipe. It leads him deep under the buildings where it is dark. Allan grips the snail that is peeking out of its shell. It looks more at ease and even curious because it had not been eaten. Then Allan's legs stop kicking as the battery dies. He pulls on the pipe again until it cracks. He sucks from the crack, filling his lungs full of air. He pulls himself along the pipe, slower now that his legs can't kick. And now the leg harness threatens to drag him down. Allan pulls on the belt. It won't unlatch. He tugs on the leg straps, but they're too tight.

He needs another breath, so he pulls on the pipe to crack it. He can't get a bubble. Below him is darkness and death. The snail doesn't even want to go there.

Allan tugs on a metal pole that frames his left leg. The motors and shock absorbers are all connected by tubes and wires. He finds a thick tube and yanks it from the left ankle piece. Air pressure is unleashed, and Allan is propelled through the water. He uses his free hand to guide himself further and further under the building. Just as the pressure spewing from the mechanical legs gives out, Allan sees a light filtering through the water. He pulls himself the rest of the way and finds the surface of the water. His head breaks into the air, and he opens his mouth to suck in the much-needed air.

The weight of Allan's mechanical legs pulls him down. He grabs the metal bar attached to his leg and pulls it up and out. The weight seems heavier than a brick of gold, and Allan's arms are so tired. Suddenly, his other leg twitches at the knee. The belt is registering more power. Disconnecting one of the legs gave the other more time. He lifts that leg easily out of the water and finds himself at the bottom of a narrow stairwell. The railing looks more like a sculpture. It goes up and down and splits and converges, but it is still a railing, and it will help him up the stairs. A single lantern at the top illuminates the steps. Water trickles down, feeding algae and moss. Spider webs span the stairwell making it obvious that these stairs have been abandoned.

"This is better than being speared by one of those hooks," Allan mutters. He uses his working leg to step up, dragging the leg that doesn't work behind him. The crazy railing is sturdy, and it braces him. One step at a time, Allan ascends.

When he gets to the spider web, Allan looks around. The web is thick. Water drops that hang on its silky thread reflect the light and bend it making the drops look like diamonds. The spider crawls out from under the ornate metal hand railing. It's larger than his fist and has thin legs three times its body length. Its little eyes look at Allan and study him.

"Come on! Get outta my way!" Allan blurts out. His voice echoes in the narrow stairwell. Responding to Allan's obvious advantages, it scuttles back into the shadow of the railing. Allan takes off the jacket he'd stolen and throws it over the web, knocking it down. He continues upward. The stars become visible, and there are only about three stories more to go. Every time he has to lift the unusable leg he wants to scream out. His arm shakes and his lower back throbs. *Keep going, just keep going.*

At the top, the fresh air fills his lungs. He's conquered the steps and is now on the roof of one of the tallest buildings. He can see most of Dantia and it is big. Hundreds of tall buildings line the horizon. They are intermingled with smaller ones, pointy ones, and some very crooked ones. Lights fill some windows, but most are dark. Allan hobbles to the edge of the roof. He can see the intersection three blocks away where he ditched the authorities. Spotlights illuminate the roads as they search desperately for Allan.

Then, as if prompted by some twisted cue, his good leg dies. He crumples onto the roof of the building. Allan's brain feels like a beaten lump of play dough. It occurs to him how impossible it will be to find Mizzi. He couldn't read his map at the mushroom forest, and now he's so far from where he should be that Mizzi won't be able to find *him*. This city is not handicapped accessible, and maybe he should have stayed in the water where it was easier to move.

Allan takes the pin-up girl pin from his pocket. When his uncle gave it to him, it had reminded him of his father. But as he touches the smooth surface, it reminds him of Rubic. Tears come to his eyes. He doesn't want Rubic to die. He did all he could to get back to him, to get help, but he has failed. Now Rubic continues to suffer because of him. *Why am I being punished?*

Allan listens to the night. All he hears is the drip of the water that runs off him. He wants to sleep, rest up, and then seek an answer. He takes the glowing snail out of his pocket. It's as bright as ever. He sets it down and watches it slowly make its way down the steps. "You've got a long way to go, but thanks for the help."

Some time later, Allan awakes to a loud thunk. He's heard that noise before. He looks up and sees Asantia's airship hovering over him. Her tow cable anchors her ship to the roof. A small door opens on the bottom of the craft and down slides Asantia on her automatic handles. She stops just above the roof and then hops down the rest of the way.

Allan moans and rolls his eyes. His luck has indeed dried up. There's not an ounce of fight left in him. "Just take me. Put me up for auction, put a collar on me or sell me for new blimp parts. I can't take anymore!" he cries. Asantia bends over him and smiles, her expressionless vitriolic and more pleasant than before. He's taken by surprise when she holds her hand and says, "Enough with the drama. I've come to help."

"What? Why?"

"Because you helped me." Asantia wears a leather vest that buttons up the sides and is stitched together from odd shaped pieces. Her pants are black and have cargo pockets below the knee bulging with who-knows-what. A large blade is strapped to her back with the handle sticking up. Allan takes her hand. She tries to lift him but fails. He collapses back onto the roof. "Oh, I'm not going anywhere, just leave me. No one can help me."

"Okay, let's cut those metal legs off. They're making you into the world's most whiny paperweight." Asantia uses her knife to cut the leg and waist straps. The metal and wire contraption falls, clattering to the roof. Asantia drags Allan to her cable by his hands and lowers the handles until Allan can reach them. Then she opens a small hatch and pulls out a harness. Allan puts the harness over his head and torso and under his butt.

"Hold on tight." She says and smiles brightly. She presses the up button. The handles hoist the two of them to her ship. When they are safe inside, the tow cable releases the roof and rolls back into her ship.

Asantia drags Allan up a narrow ramp that leads to an upper deck. Allan feels like he's a sack of potatoes. "Welcome to my flying balloon. I made it myself."

At the top of the ramp, they enter a small living space. A bin overflowing with dirty clothes is next to a cot. A dingy shower curtain decorated with little skull prints surrounds a large metal tub. A table with one chair is against the wall, covered in maps and notes. And centered next to the front window is a control panel, which is filled with levers and dials, not with lights or flashing readouts. The windows extend from ceiling to floor and surround half the room. The other half is made of fabric, patchwork walls. There are taped up drawings of animal people, flowers, patterns and designs on every wall.

"Stop eyeing my stuff. Now, you wanna get home or what?"

"That's the best thing I've heard all year. How did you find me?" Allan pulls himself up then leans his forehead on the window looking down at the city lights below. A sliver of daylight sits on the horizon.

"I've been looking for you. I didn't know where the Lorebs, those balloon creatures, took you, but I knew they were on their way to Lan Darr. They're departing souls. They travel through the Lan Darr Mountains every third night of the eighth month of the sixth year."

"Wow, that often, huh? Lucky me," Allan quips.

"Yeah, really lucky, if you think about it." She flips a lever and turns a dial. The ship starts to move.

"Wait. I need to give something to Mizzi."

"Can't. They're looking for you. If they catch me helping you, I'll be locked away for good."

Allan pulls out the key he'd gotten from Baroon and holds it up. "I need to get this to Mizzi. It'll save everyone from Jibbawk."

Asantia takes the key and inspects it. "Been busy, have you?" she hands it back. "Fine, but we do this quick. If I have to, I'll throw him the key from up here so we can make a clean getaway."

Strange Lands

Chapter 17
Carried Away

Allan takes out Mizzi's map and hands it to Asantia. It's still damp. She carefully unfolds it and lays it on her table. After looking at it a while, she flips it over. Then after looking at it some more she rotates it once and then again and grunts. Finally, a smile blooms on her face.

"I got him. He's so smart and yet, so not." She pulls a lever on her control panel, and the craft turns. The ship heads toward the edge of the city where the horizon is brightest.

"I, uh, have to ask you something." Allan bites his lip.

"Spit it out."

"I need to use the bathroom."

"What for? Swimming in the canal washed you up pretty good. You don't need a bath."

"I . . .have to pee."

"Oh. Why didn't you just say so?" Asantia puts her arms under his armpits and hauls him up with a grunt. She muscles him to a small closet next to her bed where a small round bucket sits. "No lid to sit on. I'll have to hold you."

Allan rolls his eyes. "Never mind. I'll never be able to go."

Asantia shakes her head, "Look, when you gotta go you gotta go. I don't want you bursting like an old garden hose and messing up my clean floors." She lifts him up. Allan huffs at the idea that her floors are clean. After a torturous half-minute, he goes.

Asantia returns him to the window and pats his shoulder. "Not so hard, eh?" Allan shakes his head. He's as embarrassed as it gets and wants to crawl under her cot and hide. Asantia is breathing heavily from lifting Allan but tries to hide it. She likes to be tough, though Allan wonders how tough she is. Allan's mother was tough. She'd work out at the gym three to four times a week and ran marathons twice a year. But even under her tough, rule-obsessed, high-standard personality, she was still his mom and on occasion would collapse into tears, which would drive Allan into her arms.

Asantia returns to the controls and flips a switch. "I'm sorry you can't use your legs."

"Everyone is sorry," Allan mutters, still flush with embarrassment.

"You must feel useless sometimes."

"That's putting it mildly."

"But you're not. You saved my butt. Even after I was a total fart to you. So, you're still good for some stuff." She winks at him. Now that dawn has invaded the sky, Allan can see Dantia. Far below the floating airship people walk and some fly. They're as small as ants and just as orderly. Some of the buildings are colorful.

The city looks less drab than before and mysteriously inviting like a state fair or an outdoor mall. Different flags flap from poles, and the people are wearing colorful and exotic clothing.

Allan looks up at Asantia. Light spilling in from the windows makes her shine. Her skin is soft, her hair is rich and smooth, and her golden eyes are as bright as they've ever been. He's never seen yellow eyes before. Asantia has the most beautiful eyes he's ever seen. "Are—are you from Earth?"

Asantia turns to him. "Where else would I be from?"

"I don't know. I was just . . ."

She chuckles. "I don't know if I'm from Earth. A long time ago when I was just a baby, I was found on a hilltop just south of Dantia. I didn't cry, just stared at everything. I never cried about anything."

"Really?"

"Yup. Finally, I was found and brought to Killian Crow. I was his servant for a long time. But I found his secret room. He had books and this projector that you can put moving pictures into. I would sneak in there every night and read and watch the tapes. It was strictly off-limits to slaves. Eventually, it was my turn to take the Trials." She shrugs. "I didn't do so well, but I didn't die at the Bog of Teeth." Allan avoids asking what the Bog of Teeth is. Even in his ignorance, he's confident that he'll never want to go there.

"Bit by bit, day after day, I stole supplies from Killian Crow's warehouse and his basement. Instead of sneaking into his secret room to learn stuff, I'd crawl up to the attic. I built my ship in about a year." She pulls a lever, and the ship starts to descend.

"One day, I blew the attic's roof off with black tar-cakes and filled my balloon with helium. My airship flew just like in the books I'd read. I had tried to get others to come with me, but I was the only one that had the guts." Asantia puts her fist in the air. "Been on the run ever since. They can't catch me. I'm a ghost."

The buildings get bigger as the craft lowers and makes its way to the meeting place Mizzi scribbled on his map. "Jibbawk is a ghost. The freakiest one I've ever seen."

"If you've seen Jibbawk, you're lucky to be alive," Asantia replies. She rests her fist on her hip and stares at Allan for a long while. "See, you're tougher than you look." Asantia moves from the control panel to a rusty, bent handle by the ramp doorway. She grabs the handle and cranks it around and around. Then she looks through a metal oval that protrudes from the wall and places her hand on a red button below it. After staring into the oval for a minute, she slams the red button. Nothing happens. She slams on the button again and then harder the third time. Finally, there's a hiss. The ship shudders. Asantia walks back to Allan.

"Grappling hook is set." She can see the question mark on Allan's face. "It's a bit sticky. Don't judge my ship."

Allan smiles wide. "I didn't say anything." She asks for the key. "You stay here. I'll get the key to Mizzi and be back before the fleas can bite." She winks.

Allan hands her the key. "I'd like to say goodbye.

Mizzi really helped me."

Asantia shrugs. "Send him a letter." She moves to the ramp then stops; her hand rests on the doorway for a moment. She turns. "If there were time, I'd take you to him. But there isn't. I'm sorry."

"It's okay, just tell him thank you for me."

Suddenly, there's a loud explosion. The left side of the floating ship drops. Asantia falls back and rolls all the way to Allan, landing in his lap. Another explosion jolts the ship's metal frame, and the entire ship leans further to one side. A hiss comes from the ballast balloons.

"No, you did not." Asantia cries out. She pulls herself to the controls then yanks on some levers. Nothing happens. She thrusts one lever back and forth, back and forth. "We're going down. Hold on to something!"

The craft falls through the sky turning like a Frisbee. The grappling hook still anchors the ship to the ground. The ship hits a building. The building cushions the fall somewhat, sparing Allan and Asantia's lives, but can't stop the ship from crashing to the ground. The metal frame crunches through the wall as it slips down the face of the building. A lantern on a balcony ignites the helium. Fire envelops the ship's fabric. A strange, round man-beast leaps off a bench and clears the area a moment before Asantia's ship lands on the building's frontage and slides across the lawn. It stops just before it falls into the canal. The man-beast wasn't far enough away. His hair lights on fire, and he runs away shrieking. People living in the tall building cry out and point to the burning ship; one larger woman faints.

Smoke fills up the cabin as the gears grind to a stop. Asantia grabs Allan's arms, drags him to the ramp and pushes him out the door where he falls into the canal. She dives in after him just as an explosion punctuates the destruction of her floating home. Asantia surfaces and grabs Allan's shirt. "Can you swim by yourself?"

"Yeah, I can tread water. What happened?"

"We were shot down by someone who works for Crow. Most of the authorities leave me alone, but some dangerous guys have never stopped hunting me."

"What do we do?"

"Hide."

"What?!" Allan shrieks as his eyes search his surroundings. His arms clench involuntarily as his fear threatens to immobilize him. He starts to sink, but Asantia grabs his shirt and helps him resurface. She points to an approaching boat and then starts swimming in the opposite direction. The boat is fast and wider than the other boats on the canal. It has a tall mast with a large sail filled with air. It turns as it reaches Allan and Asantia revealing Mizzi at the controls. He throws his tail toward Allan.

"Get on! Hurry! Before they see us. I've been waiting for you and you're really late."

Allan grabs hold of the tail and lets himself be pulled aboard the boat as Asantia climbs aboard. The back of the vessel arches up, and the front fèrro has been carved into the shape of an elephant. Copper and steel plates anchor the pulleys, blocks, winches, and plates that connect and hold up the tall mast. All the wood trim has intricate carvings. Inside the boat are seats in front and behind the mast. The steering tiller is at the back.

As the boat turns, the sail dumps all the air and flops like a flag. Mizzi pulls one rope tight and loosens another one. The wind fills up the sail with a loud snap, and the boat speeds through the water. Mizzi steers the boat down the wide canal and under a tall, stone bridge. The wind picks up as they near where the canal empties into a lake. The wind pushes the boat faster and faster tipping it until the side of the vessel drags in the water. The speed widens Mizzi's furry smile, which shows off his little teeth.

Alligator-like animals swarm out of a nearby side street and descend on the wreckage. Asantia sits next to Allan and watches the scavengers crawl all over her home like cockroaches over stale bread. Black columns of smoke rise from the engine of Asantia's ship and the framework sags from the heat.

"They are veskews and a lot like attack dogs," Asantia says. "But with more teeth. And they can crawl upside down and on walls and are as nasty as piranhas."

The veskews have beady eyes, large claws, and dark green scales instead of hair. They are about the size of alligators. A metal frame gives out under the weight of a veskew, and the veskew drops into the inferno below.

"See that guy?" She points to a tall bird-man following the veskews.

"I know that bird," Allan mutters. "It's the ratty-bird who caught me the first time."

Asantia pats Allan on the shoulder. "Dodged him again. He's a bad bub, that one. I've run into him on occasion. The world would be better off if he were behind bars. That's for sure. Unfortunately, he's the sheriff's brother. He'll never go to jail. The whole system is corrupt," Mizzi adds.

"They're coming!" Asantia cries out.

The veskews zero in on the boat and run on all fours toward it. They scamper over the bridge like a pack of rabid dogs. People scream and duck out of the way of the veskews, but some get trampled, and a rat-person in a fancy tailored suit gets knocked into the water.

The boat enters the lake with surprising speed for a sailboat. The water smacks the hull noisily, and its nose cuts through the small waves. The veskews skid to a stop at the shore of the lake. One jumps in the water, but instead of swimming, it thrashes around and sinks. The others pace on the shore and shriek.

After Allan can't see the veskews anymore, he relaxes. He notices Asantia still watching the column of black smoke. "Your ship is ruined because he was hunting me."

She shrugs. "It's not your fault, not really. And as for my ship? I'll make another. It was getting old anyway. Besides, we all have crap we gotta get past."

Allan sees tears in her eyes. He thought she never cried. He knew that no one could say that honestly. Her tears remove some of her make-up, and Allan can see she has little freckles underneath. In the shadow of grief and loss, she looks five years younger. What a tough life she must live. Allan thinks that she must be the same age as him.

Asantia touches his shoulder lightly and holds his

gaze for a lingering moment. She swallows hard, dabs her eyes and tries to wring out her drenched hair, all while erasing her emotions.

The boat sails parallel to the shoreline which borders with woods and rolling hills. It's quiet with the sound of lapping water and creaking sails being the only noise. Allan spies a tall step-pyramid in the distance, overgrown with plants, cracked and weather-beaten. At the top is a large door overhung with a vine-covered roof.

Allan tries to turn, but his limp legs are crumpled awkwardly in the boat. Asantia helps him pull them up and straighten them out. Mizzi sits next to Allan, while the boat maintains a course toward the pyramid. "So, you did it. I'm not surprised at all, though I got worried."

"I couldn't have done it without your mechanical legs. Can you to make me another set?"

Mizzi smiles, his whiskers angling upward. "I don't have another power source like that one. If I find one, you'll be the first to know. I wish I had a more permanent solution." His paws scratch at his large snout, and then he meticulously coils his long tail next to him.

Asantia digs out the key from her pocket and hands it over. "I think you were looking for this."

Mizzi takes the key with the furry end of his tail. "You both did good." He hops from his seat and goes back to steer the boat. He aims for the shore and crashes the boat into the sandy beach. "Nice landing," Asantia snips, picking herself off the floor.

"Not as spectacular as yours," Mizzi replies with a

smile.

"How do I get home now?" Allan asks.

"You're going to take this boat across the lake and see a bird guard named Lyllia of Meduna. She'll let you pass through a gateway. That gateway will take you home."

"Sounds easy." Allan watches Mizzi get a bag of supplies from a storage box in front of the boat, and then Mizzi returns to the back. Mizzi tosses his tail onto the beach. Allan points to the pyramid. "Jibbawk's body is up there?"

Mizzi nods. "I will lure his ghost there. When he merges with his flesh, I'll confine him and banish him to one of the outer worlds." Mizzi hugs Allan for a long while. "I'm glad we met. You're a brave one. Don't forget that." Mizzi leaps out of the boat. He turns then pushes the sailboat back into the lake. "Just cross the lake. When you get to the other side, follow the shore until you get to the House of Gold. Lyllia is there. She'll know how to get you home."

Asantia steers the boat letting the wind fill its sails. The wind is strong on the lake, but not cold. The tipping of the boat eases Allan into a reclining position, his back leaning on the side and his arms resting on the edge. He looks up at the twilight sky and bathes in the warmth of success, at peace now that he's returning home.

An hour passes. The sky is at its brightest now, which isn't that bright, especially since there is no visible sun. Allan wonders what kind of a world would get bright, but has no sun. Maybe the sun is too far away to see but would still fill up the atmosphere with light.

It is a similar world to Earth, but so different. Now that Allan isn't fighting for his life he thinks about being on another planet. He really is somewhere else. Earth isn't even in the same solar system as this planet.

"How many other worlds have you visited? Besides Earth?" Allan asks.

Asantia pulls out some food from her pocket and hands a piece to Allan. Tough and salty, it tastes like beef jerky but looks more like a sponge than a piece of meat. She hands him another piece and giggles at how he devours it. "I've been around. But I always come back here. It's my home. I've got friends here." She looks up for a moment. "The possibilities are endless in the stars. Every combination you can think of exists. Red stars, purple nights, pink mountains and ocean worlds with flying whales as big as your Earth cities. I was eaten by one of those gigantic whales and survived for two months with the people that lived between its teeth. They were super sweet to me and had a beautiful city. Day and night depended on when the whale would open its mouth."

"I'd like to see that. There are a lot of things I'd like to see, but I can't go far in a wheelchair."

"You'd be surprised at the places you can go. When you get a little older, how about I take you somewhere?"

"I'd like that. But I don't want to get eaten, no matter how friendly the whale plaque is."

"Got it. I'll pick somewhere super-snug."

"I hope 'super-snug' means cool."

Asantia laughs, "Of course it does."

"I'm confused. You were so mean to me when I

first met you. Now, you're not. It's like you're a different person."

Asantia sighs. "Look, I'm a scavenger. I do what I have to. And, I wouldn't have sold you to Killian Crow or any of the Metite Houses. Those guys are evil. I would have sold you to a Thinker. You would have worked for a year and then been given the opportunity to Test and earn your freedom."

"You know slavery is wrong, no matter what."

Asantia's eyebrows rise. "Yup. But I didn't make the rules here. There is a growing number of us who will change the rules, but it's a process. You know?"

Allan sees, in her rich yellow eyes and her radiant smile, that she is telling the truth. "So, I've meant to ask you about your tech," Allan begins. "Your world doesn't seem more advanced than Earth, but you can travel to other planets. How do you do it? How did I get here?"

Asantia adjusts the sails letting the ship pick up speed. She stands up in the boat, holding the steering tiller and a line that keeps the ship's mast standing up. The wind blows through her hair and reddens her cheeks. "Yeah, we're pretty backward here. The only reason why we have any technology at all is because of Mizzi and others like him. He's head of an underground society of thinkers and tinkers. They wrote the books that helped me make my ship. We also have a lot of books from Earth. That's why we speak English."

"But how did I get here? I was crawling through the woods."

"You must have run into a Hubbu flower. The Hubbu plant produces huge flowers that create a pollen

that creates little wormholes. Nobody knows how it works, but if you get enough pollen spores on you, they will take you through space. Mizzi thinks the pollen arrived here a long time ago and started all life in Lan Darr."

"How do you know where it takes you?" Allan asks, intrigued.

"By the color, of course. The flowers bloom in six different colors. I've blended the colors and ended up in different places. Everywhere they take you is somewhere they grow. So you don't have to worry about plopping into a world that doesn't have air or is covered in lava. It's almost as if you switch places with the pollen on the other world. That's how it feels to me."

"So you can go anywhere, anytime?"

"Well, a couple types of flowers, the deep red and the light orange ones, only bloom a few times a year. If they're not blooming, you can't go where their color leads you. I've tried to save the pollen spores for later use, but they don't keep. At some point, the spores just pop out of our world and go wherever they go."

"That's amazing. I suddenly want to plant a flower garden." Allan smiles.

Asantia winks. "They grow on Earth, too. But they are very rare. Every now and again, someone from Earth shows up. They're confused and freaked out. They'd picked the flowers and got just the right amount of pollen on them."

"Is that why there are humans here?"

"Probably. It might be why I'm here. I've wondered if that happened to me."

"I'm sorry you never met your mother or father."

"Me, too." Asantia's hair blows into her face, and she pulls it away, staring into the breeze. "Books from earth have helped us see better ways. Your books on the American system have started a revolution here."

"Wow. Good." Allan had never seen American history so clearly. "We've had our problems in the past, too."

"Yeah, but your system pushes through all these problems. You've left a golden trail for us to follow."

With all the trauma and troubles Allan has gone through, he'd almost forgotten that there were others that had similar or worse problems than him. The two continue talking for hours, laughing and sharing stories. Allan surprises himself by remembering so many good times, and Asantia's stories are nothing short of fantastic.

Finally, they reach the other side of the lake. Asantia turns and steers the vessel parallel to the shoreline. The House of Gold appears in a clearing next to a farm. It has round windows and archways overhanging doorways to courtyards and stairways. Plants of all colors and varieties hang off the balconies and overflow from hanging pots.

As they get closer, Allan sees the inlet. It's a harbor leading to a dock. On either side of the harbor entrance are two huge bird-head statues made of gold. They're fifty feet tall, or more.

Asantia passes by them and steers the boat toward a dock at the back of the harbor. The dock leads to stairs that end in a doorway. It's an over-sized doorway framed by flat golden stones that have inscriptions on them, like something from ancient Egypt.

Asantia releases the sails, so they flap in the wind. The boat slowly coasts into the small harbor and bumps into the dock. Overlooking the dock is a tall pillar with a chair at the top occupied by a fat bird that resembles an ostrich. Its feathers are green, orange and blue, similar to a parrot's. It looks old. There are no feathers on its face, which is covered in a myriad of wrinkles and spots.

"Only speak when spoken to," Asantia whispers. "I've never traveled through these gates when I had my ship, but I've heard stories of Lyllia of Meduna. If you want to get where you're going, you've got to be as polite as a monk. Otherwise, she'll send you to the far edges of the universe." Asantia looks up to the crowned, wrinkled bird. "Hello, Your Royal Highness. We wish to travel to Earth while the Earth flowers are still in bloom. Thank you for your patience and protection all these years. You look lovely today." Asantia says in her most polite tone, which sounds alien coming from her.

"Who is this with you? I don't recognize this boy," Lyllia of Meduna says.

"He is my . . ." Asantia looks at Allan for a moment then back up to Lyllia, "friend. I want to help him get home, Your Royal Highness." Asantia ties the boat to cleats in two places to keep the boat from floating away from the dock. She takes Allan's hand, pulls him to the edge and lifts him out of the boat. Then, with his arm draped over her neck and shoulders and her arm around his waist, she slowly hobbles up the steps toward the door at the top. It's a solid gold door with ornate edges and molding, large metal cross beams, and gears in the center.

Lyllia holds out a wing. "These gates are closed to all that want to pass freely. You must earn your entry. Answer this riddle and you shall pass:

A natural state, I'm sought by all.

Go without me, and you shall fall.

You think of me after you spend,

and erode me when you eat to no end.

If you go too slow or too fast

you will not last.

What am I?"

Lyllia of Meduna leans back in her chair. "What does that mean?" Allan asks. He isn't in the mood for games.

"How should I know? I've never heard of answering a riddle to use the gates," Asantia complains then sets Allan at her feet so she can rest.

"You have fifteen flips of my coin." Lyllia tosses a large gold coin up in the air. It flips and shimmers, its reflection flashing like a strobe light. Then she catches it. "One." Then flips again.

Allan puts his hands on his head. He can't blow this chance. This door will lead him home. Without Asantia's ship or spending days collecting flowers, it is his fastest way home. "Okay, a natural state, I'm sought by all. Go without me, and you shall fall. You think of me after you spend, and erode me when you eat to no end. If you go too slow or too fast, you will not last." Allan thinks for a long moment. Lyllia flips the gold coin for the sixth time.

"What's a natural state? Happy? Yes, people want to be happy," Allan thinks out loud.

"But you can't spend happiness," Asantia argues. They are deep in thought as the ninth flip turns in the air.

"Erode me when you eat to no end. What does that mean?" Allan grunts and smacks his hand on the step in frustration. Sweat trickles down his cheek.

Flip twelve.

"What are you? You're an idiot; that's what," Asantia mumbles to herself. She's staring off at the lake.

Allan's eyes pop open. "It's balance. That's the answer, balance. Your Royal Highness, it's balance."

"Nope," says Lyllia of Meduna. "It is greed." She flips the coin in the air and catches it. "I just earned a nice little commission for stalling you."

An arch over the gateway door is topped by a balcony filled with odd looking plants and some wind chimes that start ringing out. Allan looks at them because something catches his eye.

A column of black rises and twists like a tornado. The movement of the black is familiar. Beetles. The tornado bends at the top and lowers to the stairway, slowly forming into Jibbawk. It blocks Allan's way home.

Strange Lands

Chapter 18
Poison in the Water

Rubic stands in front of a crowd of people whose faces he can't quite make out in the dark even with all their lanterns and flashlights. Thick bandages wrap around his forehead and neck, and his arm is in a blue sling. It has been sixteen hours since the flood, the last time Rubic had seen Allan alive.

Two rangers stand next to Rubic. A short, rotund ranger with a mustache speaks into a walkie-talkie. The other ranger, tall and solid, organizes the group into halves. The left half, eight people total, is an Amish family. They wear similar clothing. The women sport blue dresses, white aprons, capes, and bonnets. The men have coats, straight-leg pants, and wide-brimmed hats. Rubic thanks Larry for alerting the family. When they heard a child had gone missing, they rushed to help.

"Wittmer family, you take the north side of the river," the tall ranger orders. The other half of the crowd numbers fifteen. They're not Amish but a menagerie of characters as diverse as patrons in truck stops and roadside diners.

"The rest of you take the south side." With that

last order, the group begins the search. Flashlights and lanterns dance in the forest like colossal fireflies.

The rotund Ranger turns to Rubic. Thick eyebrows shelter his deep-set eyes. "We'll find him. This is the fastest search party ever assembled. Thanks to Larry."

Larry smiles and swats the air toward the short ranger. "No trouble. I've been delivering mail up here for twelve years. Yup, I knew who would come an' help."

The tall Ranger listens to chatter on his radio. "We'll also have dogs out here within two hours. Don't worry; we'll find Allan. He couldn't have gone far."

Rubic nods and smiles even though he's worried. "He can't even walk," he mutters. The tall Ranger hands water bottles to Rubic and Larry.

"Why don't you think he was washed farther downstream than you were?" the rotund ranger asks.

Rubic shakes his head. "He was with me for some time. Had to have been. When I woke up, he'd built a dam around me. It diverted the water, so I'd stay dry. It would've taken a while to build."

"Okay. We'll search downstream, but not too far. Our search pattern will include a five-mile radius from where you woke up."

Larry pats Rubic on the back. "Sounds like Allan's a smart cookie, yup. Maybe he's made himself a lean-to and passed out for the night. It is late."

Past one o'clock in the morning, twenty hours have passed since the flood. Rubic isn't naive. Being lost for this long is not good. He starts to hike up the river and Larry follows.

"Try not to worry too much," Larry says. "How

much trouble could he get into?"

"I'm worried about how much trouble can find *him*. There are bears up here, and mountain lions, AND moose. Don't moose trample things? What if a horde of bees has stung him? There are timber rattlesnakes up here, too. Jeez." Rubic calls out, "ALLAN!" No response. Allan's name echoes off the trees, and the ferns shimmer in the cool night air.

"He's in more trouble than just being lost," Rubic concludes after walking for some time. He sweeps his light over rocks and inside bushes and fern clusters and under logs. "His parents died not long ago. I can tell he's on the verge of losing interest in his life. He won't speak to anyone, not even me."

"Sounds like a normal reaction to a terrible thing."

"Some things that have happened to him are *more* than terrible." Rubic starts to cry. He does nothing to impede the trail of tears tumbling over his cheek and melding into his beard hair.

"The curse of humanity is the things we can think. Our minds can be so creative and so haunted at the same time. We must follow the light at all costs. Keep the darkness behind us. It may change and evolve. It will still try to get our attention, but if we keep looking forward, the dark will eventually be forgotten." Larry says as he sweeps his light over dark bushes and numerous trees that look like telephone poles.

"It takes so long to forget. You know kids. You've got a couple. Time goes by much slower for them. Allan has been gone for a long time, but to him, it must feel like a hundred years."

Rubic shines a light on the trunk of a tree. He sees the red clay left by the raging flood. He wipes his finger on the clay. His finger collects a clump. "You say this flood happens every so often?"

"Yup, ever since they dammed the lake at the top and the glacier started melting. First one was in the mid-fifties." Larry points his light at the tree. "Looks like the flood left a high water mark on all the trees."

"Yeah, but..." Rubic's mind is puzzled. He's not a scientist of any sort, but he cannot shake the feeling that the clay is not a typical effect of flooding. He smells the clay on his finger then tastes it. He spits as fast as his muscles can retch. "Whoa! That's weird." His tongue starts tingling.

"What is it?" Larry scrapes his own red clay from the tree trunk and puts it up to his nose.

"Don't taste it. Something's not right with the clay."

"It's dang red. Most clay has iron in it that gives it a red hue, but this is rather bright. My Lord." Larry stares at the red clay on his fingers, his brow furled.

"It has a metallic taste. Very bitter. And my whole tongue is numb now." He measures the height of the waterline on the tree trunk. "Has it ever flooded this high? The water line's probably four feet up."

"Don't know. The lake holds quite a lot of water. I'm sure it's normal."

"Okay, the amount of water's normal, but what was *in* the water sure isn't."

"Yup, I would agree with you on that, pardner."

Chapter 19
Light in the Dam

Rubic and Larry follow the river to the campsite and his overturned truck. The Wittmer family and some others have finished their search and had returned to the camp empty-handed. The painkillers Rubic took have made him too weak to keep searching. His arm aches. His ribs thump. And deep breaths send shocks of pain throughout his chest. He'll need to go to the hospital soon, but he refuses to leave with Allan still missing. To keep himself occupied while the dogs and the others finish their search, Rubic collects some of his gear from the mud. After placing a folding chair, a bag of clothes and his washed-out lantern on a pile, he arranges for the Wittmer family to tip his truck back on its tires. They succeed easily. The roof is bent and slightly crumpled, and the windshield is shattered, but there is still enough headroom to sit. The truck starts and runs then sputters and dies. With a heavy sigh, Rubic shuffles to the tailgate and, after popping the handle and lowering the gate, sits heavily.

A female ranger walks up to him. Rubic recognizes her. "You're the ranger that tried to kick Allan and me off my campsite."

She shrugs. "You should have listened to me. There's a reason we do what we do. We're not the bad guys."

Rubic looks away for a moment then back to her. "I guess so. I apologize."

She sits next to him. "How are you feeling?" she asks. Her eyes are kind despite their previous encounter.

Rubic rubs his face, which tingles like he's covered in tiny bugs. "Not fine. I'm getting sicker by the minute. The pain isn't bad, but I'm starting to see things. Like light trails. I can feel my heart thumping in my veins like there's a marching band inside me."

"Well, I've more medical training than the other Rangers. Let me look at you." She takes his pulse and looks into his eyes. "Your adrenaline is working its way out of your body, but you're still in shock. I think it would be good to let me take you to the hospital now."

Rubic shakes his head. "Not yet. I can handle this. What I *need* is to find my nephew." Rubic stands. He watches a truck pull up to the campsite. Two men unload the dogs from the back of the truck and head out.

She touches his shoulder. "The dogs will find him. It will be okay. I'll stay with you."

Rubic shakes his head and follows the dogs, Alice keeping up with him. "They gave me a handful of ibuprofen earlier, but it feels like morphine."

"Morphine is a little too strong to have in the first aid kit." The female ranger stops Rubic and puts her wrist up to Rubic's forehead. "You feel hot."

"I *feel* hot. Like, I-want-to-rip-my-shirt-off hot."

She giggles. "Now we wouldn't want you to do that."

"What is your name? I . . . Forgot it," Rubic asks.

"Alice," she says.

"Alice, what else can I be doing? This shouldn't be taking so long. He can't use his legs. Where could he have gone? "

"I don't know." Alice takes his hand and holds it tightly. "We need to let the dogs find him. They're faster at this than we are. We don't need to follow them."

Rubic shakes his head. "Something isn't right. It doesn't fit. Allan should've been found a dozen yards from where I woke up. I know these mountains like the back of my hand. But Allan, he's never even *been* here before."

"He's young. Probably trying to get help. He could have dragged himself a long way."

Hours later, two dozen people or more with flashlights and lanterns return to the campsite. Hound dogs return as well. No one has had any luck.

The little ranger fiddles with his hat and approaches Rubic. "The search stalled at the base of a steep incline where the river flattens out. The water line on the trees was so low it would not have swept Allan any further."

"Why can't the dogs find him?" Rubic snaps as he sways back and forth.

"You need to sit down. That's order." Alice helps Rubic to a large, fallen tree trunk.

The rotund ranger approaches with a brown dog with white patches over his ears and friendly eyes. "Gary here's a tracking dog. He's trained to find specific scents. You don't have any of Allan's things, so we were never able to get him a clear sample to smell. I'm sorry."

"Arrrrrrr! Allan! You get out here right now, or you're grounded." Rubic cries out. He looks up at the stars. He can see the span of the Milky Way above him. The stars seem to dance and move around. They make patterns that rotate like those in a kaleidoscope.

"And why is everything looking so funny?" Rubic says. He looks at all the characters that have come to help. "This is like a carnival show," he mutters and starts to laugh for no reason at all.

"Our search radius has more territory to the right because we assume Allan would try for the road." Alice looks puzzled.

When Rubic doesn't stop laughing Alice pulls his chin down and shines her light in his eyes. "Your eyes are really dilated. Dilated pupils can indicate head trauma." She inspects the other eye. "Unless you're on drugs you haven't told me about. You need to go to the hospital. I'll have to insist."

"Not without Allan."

"Dilated pupils can be the result of severe, potentially life-threatening conditions. You could have an intracranial hematoma, ruptured brain aneurysm, or have high intracranial pressure."

Rubic slowly looks around. He waves his flashlight back and forth. He shines his light at the crowd of searchers. One of them has a horse. It's huge, looks furry and has a funny nose. The saddle shimmers in the light. Rubic knows he's seeing things differently, so he shakes his head vigorously. He sees a strange pattern in his vision. The leaves of a nearby bush look like a thousand clapping hands. *What?! This is unreal.* He squints and the hands dissolve into normal leaves. There are noises off in the distance and a faint sound of cheering. Rubic runs his hand through his hair. "I'm hallucinating."

"You took drugs?" Alice exclaims.

"No. But I feel funny, and I'm seeing things that aren't real." He remembers the taste of the red clay. "I've ingested poison."

Alice takes his wrist and checks his pulse. "Your heartbeat has quickened. What did you eat?"

"Clay." Rubic stands. He pulls Alice along toward the horse. When he gets closer, the shadow that made it look like it was furry like wooly mammoth fades.

"If you were poisoned you need to go to the hospital now. I'll take you there." Alice pleads. Her hands reach out and grab Rubic's arm, but he pulls away.

"I only tasted the clay."

"What clay?"

Rubic shows her a tree trunk. She scrapes some clay off the trunk and smells it. "I see what you mean. This has a chemical odor I've never smelled before. It burns my nasal passageway."

Rubic rubs his temples trying to focus his mind. "We know the water came from the dam. The lake must've spilled a ton of water. Larry told me a flood had occurred a long time ago when a piece of the glacier broke off and landed in the river. It must've happened again. Maybe twice."

"That's right. It has to be an overflow."

"But this clay has to have come from somewhere. If it's poison, then it had to be in the water."

"Illegal dumping?"

"Allan can't go anywhere. Not really. Not fast enough to get this lost. Something's wrong." Rubic snaps his fingers. "My brother, Allan's father, told me about Occam's Razor. It's a theory on deduction." Rubic paces as he thinks out loud. Unnatural energy pulses through his veins. "We must shave off as many assumptions as possible. What is left is the simplest solution."

"Which is what?" Alice asks.

"Allan was taken away."

"We're in communication with local authorities. If someone had found him, we'd know about it. You thinking he was abducted?"

"The clay and how it's poisoning me is connected to Allan's disappearance. I can feel it. Anything else is too coincidental." Rubic looks at the dark mountainside. "Someone might want to cover up illegal dumping in the lake, which would be investigated if Allan was found sick from poison." He rubs his eyes. "Take me to the dam."

"The road's been washed out for years. It's condemned. Fenced off. No way could anyone get there. Come on. You're tired. Let's take a minute to think this through. What you're saying is impossible."

Rubic doesn't listen to her and stumbles up to the man holding the horse. He's an Amish man with a long beard and a white shirt. "I need your horse. Please."

The Amish man nods quietly and hands Rubic the lead rope. Rubic tries to put his foot in the stirrup but is seeing double.

"Where are you going?" Alice yells.

"Are you coming?" He finds the stirrup and steps up. He flops awkwardly onto the saddle. The horse steps back protesting.

Alice pushes Rubic's right foot over the saddle. "Scoot back, now," Alice orders. She steps up and settles onto the front of the saddle careful not to kick Rubic.

Rubic, glad for her help, hugs her waist tightly. Her warmth helps him to relax. Alice snaps the reins, and they gallop away. He closes his eyes not wanting to suffer from any more hallucinations, but a kaleidoscope of colors teases the insides of his eyelids.

The two ride hard for over an hour. The forest gets thick again, and the temperature drops. Rubic's butt is numb, and he feels like he's sitting on cold T-bone steaks. Alice maneuvers the horse as close to the river as possible. The walls of the canyon get closer to the river the higher they ride, and the river gets deeper. As the horse rounds a bend in the canyon, they see the dam. The moonlight illuminates the concrete megastructure. The enormity of the structure makes Rubic suck in his breath. The dam is a monolith in the dark that towers above their heads. It spans the canyon and has support ribs that segment the sloping wall. At the top of the dam is a series of spillways. One of them is open, letting the water run out and down the dam wall, feeding the river. The other three are closed but dripping. On the right side of the dam is an old, concrete control house. It has six small windows along its flat front, is built on a solid concrete foundation next to the river and extends into the cliff side. Further to the right, a large, white pipe comes out of the cliff and turns. Water trickles from the pipe and filters through the gravel and back to the river.

Alice pets the side of the horse's sweaty neck. "Almost there, girl," she whispers to the horse. She snaps the reins and rides up the rough side of the embankment where the service road used to be. The horse clambers up the side until it gets to the original road. Rubic shines his light on the pavement. Grasses thrust up from the cracks in every available space, but some are flattened and broken at the stems.

"Truck tracks," Alice says pointing to the road. "If someone does have Allan, we need to wait for the authorities. I've already called them so they'll be here shortly."

"No. Allan's in trouble. We go now. You can stay back if you want. Just tell me how to get into the dam."

"Fine, I'll go with you. I'm not supposed to let you out of my sight. Besides, I'm the one with the medical training."

Alice slows the horse as she nears the large dripping pipe. Rubic falls off the saddle and barely lands on his feet. He looks at the water exiting the pipe.

"It smells just like the red clay, only stronger." He shines the light on the pipe. The red clay has built up on the walls of the pipe. More water starts coming out of the pipe. Rubic backs up so he won't get wet.

"Rubic," Alice says. "Look." There's a single light on in one of the windows above them.

Chapter 20
The Bait Always Gets Eaten

Asantia grabs Allan's hand and drags him back down the steps to the dock. The beetles scramble in circles as Jibbawk slides down the steps as if it were floating. Allan holds Asantia's hand with a vice-like grip. His mind races. The doorway to home is right behind that creature. He's so close, but not close enough. Frustration burns hot inside Allan, and if only he could channel the energy, he'd have a lethal flamethrower at his disposal.

Jibbawk aims a long pointy finger, which looks like a solid, black claw, at Allan. Red fluid drips from the point like a leaky hypodermic needle. The beetles skittle and move, making wet clicking sounds.

"Sss, I want the key, and I will tear through your body to get it." Jibbawk's red eyes widen, showing off glowing pupils.

"I, I don't have it. I gave it away," Allan squeaks.

"I can sssmell it on you. It'sss in your pocket."

Allan pats his back pocket. The key is in there. But he gave it to Mizzi. Allan's mind races. "I . . . gave it away. There's nothing in my pocket," Allan says defiantly, though his voice quivers.

"You're a terrible liar." Jibbawk's dagger-shaped finger gets closer to Allan.

"Back off, Jibbawk, and take your dung beetles with you. Otherwise, I'll slice you into six pieces," Asantia snaps. Her fingers on her free hand reach up to the handle of her long knife strapped to her back.

Jibbawk lunges for Allan's throat. Asantia whips out her blade and hacks at Jibbawk.

The blade moves through the beetles causing zero damage. In retaliation, the beetles leap onto the blade and bite at Asantia's hand, forcing her to let go. Jibbawk slashes at Asantia with his claws. They tear her leather shirt and slice her skin. She cries out, loses her balance and falls off the dock and into the water. Allan pulls the key from his back pocket and holds it up. "Take it. Just leave us alone!"

Jibbawk snatches the key from Allan. It grabs him by the throat and hauls him up and off the dock. *Choking. Can't breathe. Pain.* Beetles swarm all over Allan and bite his skin, and it feels like lightning envelops him. A scream bursts from his throat. Allan grabs at Jibbawk, his hand seizing beetles. They bite him and draw blood, but Allan doesn't care. He wants to rip Jibbawk apart. His fists close around the beetles, and he crushes them, but it only makes Jibbawk laugh.

The wind comes suddenly. Over the top of the golden house comes a small helicopter. It looks like a copper teacup: the handle supports the black, belching motor and swishing blades. Under the helicopter dangles a metal shape. It's cylindrical with a glass door on top. Inside is the prostrate body of Jibbawk. It's similar to his beetle shape, but not made of beetles. Its body is completely covered in spines. The exposed skin around its eyes, beak and legs are pale and bluish. Its leathery hands lay clasped across its chest. Jibbawk looks at the helicopter and then looks at his body encased in the cylinder. It marvels at its former flesh and blood.

Mizzi grips the controls tightly. He speaks into a crooked metal pipe with a flange on the end that projects his voice over the whirr of the blades.

"I have something you need." The helicopter lowers the cylinder to the steps carefully. "Just don't hurt the boy *or* the girl and you can have it."

Jibbawk tosses Allan into the water like he's a doll. The beetles fall off Jibbawk and skitter up the steps in a stream of a thousand shining shells. They leap onto the cylinder. The glass cracks under the weight until the pressure is so great that it shatters. The beetles cover Jibbawk's dead body. They melt away like frost when it meets the sun. It only takes a moment more before Jibbawk sits up, looks at its body, and stands. Its claws are gone, having been replaced by articulate fingers with sharp nails and has quills. Long quills adorn its neck like a collar, and short quills cover every other part of its body.

"YYYYEEESSSSSSS!" Jibbawk screams. "I'm back! I'm flesh. I can feel my bonesss, I have quillsss again and a tongue in my beak. I am more powerful than I ever wasss." Its quills spread out like a chicken fluffing its feathers. It plucked one from its forearm and licked the end. "I have enough poison in these quillsss to kill a thousand Hetaphantsss."

The gateway at the top of the stairs opens. A wind, a powerful vacuum, is sucked into the doorway. A dusty darkness containing the spores of the Hubbu plant lies beyond the threshold. Jibbawk isn't holding on to anything. Its feet are yanked out from under it, and in one slippery movement, Jibbawk is sucked into the doorway. Lyllia of Meduna quickly closes the door with a pull of a lever.

Mizzi lands the helicopter on the dock. He helps Allan out of the water, and then they help Asantia.

"You did well, Allan."

"Yeah, yeah, so what was hiding the key on Allan all about?" Asantia demands.

"I had to use you to lure Jibbawk here. It was the only way to get it close to the gateway."

"You lied to me. I thought you needed the key," Allan huffed.

"The key gave Jibbawk something to follow. I needed it to believe that the key was its only hope."

"I was bait!"

"You saved a lot of people in this world, Allan. You're a hero," Mizzi says to lighten Allan's mood.

"Two minutes later and Jibbawk would have popped off Allan's head like it was a dead flower bud." Water drips off Asantia's hair and body.

"Did you mean all that stuff you said?" Allan asks Mizzi. "Are we friends or did you just need me and now I'm useless?"

"Sometimes good people use each other. They'll do it to protect people, to spare feelings, or for the greater good. I'm sorry, I truly am. But I am still your friend and am in great debt to you. Jibbawk is ten thousand light years away on a moon called Plethiomia. It's a very dangerous place with many large beasts, much larger and stronger than Jibbawk. We won't see Jibbawk on this, or any other world, ever again. When you couldn't walk anymore, you thought you were useless. A burden. But you know that isn't the case. You can still do great things."

Allan rubs his sore neck. "I get it. I'm not helpless. I've still got my hands, my eyes and my brain."

Mizzi gives Allan a high five. "You just passed your Testing. You're free now."

Lyllia starts clapping. "Thank you, Allan. Soon, everyone will hear what you've done. You'll never have to fear walking the streets of Dantia ever again."

"I guess I like being a bait-hero. It's nice." Allan blushes. Asantia helps Allan to the top of the stairs, seats him in front of the door like a package and then looks at Lyllia still sitting in her chair like a queen.

"Can we go, Your Royal Highness? Even though we got the riddle wrong?"

Lyllia smiles and pulls a different lever. "You didn't get that wrong. It *was* Balance. There is a balance to all. How you rise or how you fall. From the life you live, to the money you give. You did marvelously. When I let Jibbawk hide in my balcony, I knew of Mizzi's alchemy. Oh, I could not let you be right because I had filled the gateway with pollen that went to Plethiomia. Trust me; you don't want to go there."

Asantia grips a gold handle next to the doorway, bracing herself. The doorway opens with a swoosh of air.

Wind sucks into the room.

"Your Royal Highness, are you sure you're not sending me to where Jibbawk just went?" Allan yells over the noise of rushing air.

Lyllia scowls from her high perch. "I do not simply open doors, young boy. This gate is not a toy. It will take you home."

Asantia bends down and kisses Allan on his cheek. "Anyone else would have left me to fall into the crack during that earthquake. You didn't. Thanks for saving me." Her yellow eyes seem electric, her smile soft and her lips full and red.

"You, too," Allan replies, holding on to the top step of the stairs. "See you soon? You promised to take me somewhere cool."

"Yeah I did. When you're eighteen, I'll come see you." Asantia's hair dances in the rushing wind.

"Deal!"

Allan lets go of the step and slides through the doorway into the dark room. A dozen glass doors line walls on either side and behind the doors are rows after rows of flowers. The door in front of the blue flowers opens, exposing the pollen to the sucking air. The pollen swirls into the room, sparking like static electricity and surrounds him. His body jerks to the left, then the right. Something pulls on Allan's skin. Even his teeth feel tugged. His body jerks up then down; then everything goes dark.

Chapter 21
Waterslide at a Zoo

Rubic and Alice crouch down and run as light-footed as possible to the door of the dam's control house. Rubic gets to the door first. It's locked. He turns to the rocky cliff side and grabs a stone the size of a football. He brings the rock down on the door handle until it breaks. The door opens into a long hallway. Moonlight spills into the building illuminating the greenish stained walls. There are three closed doors on the interior sidewall and one door at the back. Rubic turns to Alice, looking at her belt. "I suddenly feel like I should have a gun." She did not have one.

"You couldn't shoot straight in your condition anyway."

Rubic finds a branch. It's not as thick as he wanted, but it will have to do. Holding the stick up like a baseball bat, Rubic tiptoes into the building.

Rubic knows Allan is in here; he can feel it. Small pebbles and dried mud crunch under Rubic's feet. He tries the first door handle. It's locked. He considers busting it open, but when he removes his hand from the knob, he notices his fingers have wiped a thick layer of dust from the handle. No one has been in this room for quite a while. He checks the other two doors. Same dust. He moves to the last door. This handle is clean.

"Are you sure you should go in there?" whispers Alice.

"I'm as sure as the sun will rise." Rubic pulls open the door. A swoosh of wind makes a 'suuuca' sound. Rubic feels cool air on his cheeks and sees a dim light. The room is an office with a desk, a bookshelf and a wall full of filing cabinets. There is no dust on any of the surfaces, yet the room doesn't look used. The desk is missing a computer, papers, pens, and other essential office supplies. There isn't even a chair.

Rubic leads Alice through the office to a far door. The dim light shines from under the door and looks wavy in Rubic's altered vision. He rubs his eyes and turns the handle slowly then bashes the door open with his shoulder, trying to catch anyone inside by surprise. The door whips open and bangs against the wall.

The room is huge, warehouse huge. A metal stairway off to the left leads to a catwalk. Three huge metal pipes protrude from the back wall and then bend ninety degrees to the floor. They must be turbines, one of which is on and generating power. Huge black cables run from the generator to an air conditioning unit that sits on top of a large metal box, which is almost as large as a shipping container. It must be a walk-in freezer. Along the exterior wall are tables clustered with beakers, books, jugs of chemicals, centrifuge machines, computers, notepads and shelves full of stuff.

"Allan!" Rubic yells as he steps into the room ready to swing his stick. "Allan!"

Dogs bark and banging echoes throughout the laboratory from somewhere farther inside the building. Rubic turns around to see Alice. His eyes widen. She's still in the doorway, her face tight and angry, her hand holding the handle tight.

Her lips are pressed together. "I'm sorry Rubic. But neither you nor anyone else can stop me. My work is too important. I'm on the brink of discovery here. People have polluted entire ecosystems for less."

Rubic shakes his head in disbelief. "*Your* work?"

"I lost a daughter. Seventeen years ago, she vanished into thin air. We were in a field of the most beautiful flowers you've ever seen. She was in her vintage bassinet. It was white with a green vine painted along the side. I turned my back for a second, Rubic. A second." she spat. "It was the flowers. They took her somewhere. It took me years, but I've found a flower. Just one and I isolated the compound and have been testing the chemical reaction for years. I'm so close, you know." She huffed. "I believe the flowers have taken Allan, too."

"Flowers? Take a person? What are you talking about?" Rubic questions whether he's hearing Alice right or hallucinating her speaking to him. "This is crazy. What you're saying is so impossible."

"I know. No one will believe me. That's why I have to succeed first. I have to find out how the flowers work. Soon, you will understand me. When Allan is never found, when they scour this mountain and find nothing, you will understand my pain." Alice takes

off her hat and tosses it at Rubic's feet. "Never fit me anyway. Goodbye, Rubic. There is a way out, deeper in the dam. I hope you get to it before it is too late. I just need a head start." She slams the door shut then uses her key to engage a deadbolt.

Rubic runs to the door. "What did you do to Allan? Hey! You psycho." He slams on the door with his fists. Anger forces his jaw shut. He feels like he's going to explode.

Alice doesn't answer. Rubic spins around and presses his back to the door. He's confused. *So all this laboratory stuff is hers. What is she doing that is so important she had to dump tons of chemicals in the lake? What does it have to do with her missing daughter? What flowers is she talking about? Allan has to be in here. There is no other place for him to go.*

A red light catches Rubic's eye. It's from a square object sitting by the wall. Rubic leans close to the object, which looks like a pile of clay the size of a deck of cards. The clay is wrapped in cellophane with a timer secured to it with duct tape. It's a bomb. His eyes follow wires down the wall. There's another explosive fifty feet away, then another. This whole place is rigged to explode.

Rubic runs to the middle the room. Dogs yip and bark incessantly from some other room. "Allan!!!" He searches the makeshift laboratory. Rubic runs to the cooler behind the turbine pipes. He yanks the door open and peers inside. His panic overwhelms him. He runs into the cooler. "Allan! You in here?" He gets to the back wall. No Allan.

How long has it been? How much time do I have?

Rubic, ignoring his injuries, bolts from the cooler and runs up the stairs taking two at a time. The metal catwalk along the lakeside of the wall goes under the large turbine pipes. At the far end is a door. He runs to it not concerned with his heaving breathing or time-bomb ticking heart.

The door is unlocked. Beyond the door are cages, lots of them. They line a tunnel that heads deep into the dam, imprisoning dogs, monkeys, rats, rabbits and birds. They're all going nuts: barking, jumping, flapping and shrieking. "Allan! Are you in here?" Rubic almost leaves but remembers Alice's words. She said there is a way out, deep in the dam. It has to be here. He runs down the seemingly endless row of animal cages. Six or seven cages at the far end have toppled over; all but one is still occupied by noisy birds. One large cage lies open, its hinge broken and bent. Rubic expects to run into a wild, crazed dog or orangutan, but doesn't.

Rubic follows a trail with his eyes—a trail of spilled cereal and birdseed that goes to an open drain on the floor at the end of the tunnel. The drain is four feet across and centered underneath three basketball-sized metal pipes coming out of the wall and turning down into the floor. Each pipe has a large red valve wheel attached to it. Rubic inspects the drain. A glint of light catches his eye. It's a pin. He picks it up and cradles the pin in his palm. It's the 50's pin-up girl he'd fastened to Allan's shirt. He *was* here but escaped. "Allan! Are you down there? Please, say something!!" The drain leads into the heart of the dam. It's dark and damp, and it smells like the poison that covers the canyon below. It's large enough for Allan's body, but it must be a long way down. The darkness from the pipe seems to reach out as if it has fingers that can grab and take. Rubic remembers the pipe he passed on his way to the control house. It's the same diameter and came from the same side of the dam. It has to be the same pipe. But if it isn't, Allan might be trapped down there. How could he know? He's got to think fast. This building is going to blow any second.

Rubic runs to the nearest cage and grabs it by the top handle. He drops it down the pipe and listens. It goes a long way down. After he hears it clatter at the bottom, he hears the bird screech. Rubic drops all the birdcages down the tube, takes each rabbit and rat and dumps them down into the hole. He looks at the dog and monkey cages. They're too big to pick up. He runs by each cage and opens the doors. When he turns, he's staring at growling dogs. The monkeys have already headed toward the drain. Rubic kicks an empty cage at the dogs. "Get! Get to the drain, you fleabags." The dogs back up. When the dogs get too close to the monkeys, the monkeys choose to leap into the drain. Rubic kicks the cage one more time forcing the dogs into the drain. They yip all the way to the bottom. "At least you're not going to be blown to bits." Rubic yells. He steps over the cage and looks into the dark hole.

An explosion rocks the walls. Then another. Then another. Rubic turns to the door and sees a ball of fire. He closes his eyes and jumps into the darkness. The speed of his fall surprises him as his stomach threatens to leap out of his throat. "*Too fast, too fast, too fast!*"

Rubic screams. He braces for an impact that will surely break something in his body.

Allan feels himself rolling and turning in the same way he rolled and turned in the flood. He can't breathe or hear any sound.

Then his body hits gravel. Water washes over him. It's that bitter chemical water. It's nighttime, and the moon is high overhead. One moon surrounded by familiar stars. He's home. The night is cool, and the crickets chirp loudly, all are oddly comforting because of their familiarity. He sees the dam stretch across the canyon and the control house built into the side of the mountain. And there's light. Allan remembers his ultimate goal—to get help for his trapped uncle. Maybe it's not too late.

Clattering echoes down the pipe he just emerged from, rattling louder and louder until it stops. He looks into the dark, straining to see. A parrot bursts out of the pipe, flapping and screeching. It lands on Allan's face, and he falls back.

He hears another clanging in the pipe. Two wire cages burst out of the pipe and land on him. He hears more noise coming down the chute and rolls away from the opening. Two more bird cages. Allan sees them piling up and pulls the cages from the end of the pipe to allow more to tumble out. The cages are full of parrots and crows and pigeons. Another cage breaks open, and a bird goes flying away. *Are these cages and animals from Lan Darr?* Rabbits and rats fly out. They're unhurt, and they scatter.

Then comes screeching. Out fly a monkey and an orangutan. They land and run. Then out fly dogs. It's like a water slide at a zoo.

As if being surrounded by wounded animals of all kinds isn't weird enough, the control house explodes. Allan thinks he is far enough away not to be in danger, so he watches. There is another explosion. The orange plume rises like a bubble under water; only it's massive and hot. Allan flinches as a third explosion takes out the entire side of the control house.

A visible crack snakes its way up the side of the dam, and water shoots out. Now Allan is in danger. He's going to be flooded out, again. His body races with adrenaline, and he's so afraid.

Snap. Crack.

More thuds come from the pipe. A man flies out. The man lands in the gravel and rolls. When he comes to a stop, his head pops up. Rubic! Tears burst from Allan's eyes, and he sobs in an expulsion of pent up emotion.

"Allan! My God!" Rubic leaps to his feet, slipping on the gravel. He scoops Allan up and hugs him hard. Allan coughs between sobs.

Snap. The crack in the dam widens. The spray of water turns into a roaring torrent. Rubic lifts Allan and follows the monkeys uphill.

"Rubic, the birds." Allan screams.

Rubic turns to the pile of cages, rips open them all and then shakes them, so the birds fly out the doors. He returns to Allan, picks him up and runs up the gravel slope.

They get to a steep hillside. Rubic, in his adrenaline-fueled panic, bad arm and all, pulls Allan over his shoulder like a sack of potatoes and clambers up the slippery, pine needle-strewn incline.

A huge chunk of concrete collapses to the riverbed and causes a catastrophic failure in the structure. The entire dam ruptures and a million gallons of water flood the valley. It's more water than the earlier flash flood, a lot more.

Rubic can't go higher. Even the monkeys have stopped climbing. Rubic turns and slowly lets Allan slide from his shoulders. The water rushes below. They're safe from its clutches.

Rubic gasps, trying to catch his breath. He turns and grabs Allan and hugs him. "Damn good timing." Rubic sees Allan is still crying and lets himself cry also. "Are you okay?"

"I'm okay, really," Allan says through sobs.

Rubic can hardly believe he's sitting next to Allan, listening to his nephew. "You can speak!"

Allan wipes his nose on his t-shirt. "I'm fine, better now. I'm so tired and I'm shaky, but I feel okay."

The orangutan makes a 'hea hea' sound and starts picking at its teeth. The black monkey paces on the ledge looking down at the destruction and contaminated lake water rushing by.

Rubic hugs Allan again. "Aw man, I was so worried. How in the H-E-double-hockey-sticks did you get here? Did some lady bring you up here? What did she do to you?"

Allan remembers Asantia, Lan Darr and the city of Dantia. He remembers Mizzi and his mechanical legs. He smiles when he thinks of Lithic Fury Baroon and he remembers Jibbawk.

"I went somewhere else for a while. Somewhere strange and far away."

"I'll bet," Rubic states, realizing how much more exposure to the poison Allan must have had.

"We need to get you to the hospital ASAP." Rubic watches the water slowly lower as the lake spills down the mountainside. "But we're gonna be stuck here for a while."

Suddenly, a black helicopter whips up the night breeze. As it lowers, the chopping blades become audible. A man in an orange jacket rappels from the helicopter wearing night vision goggles. He lands on the ledge.

"Rubic?" he shouts over the whirring helicopter blades.

"Yeah. And this is Allan."

"We're gonna get you out of here. One at a time."

"Allan first."

The helicopter lowers a rescue bucket, and they strap Allan in. Allan rises to the helicopter unable to take his eyes off Rubic who can't keep his eyes off Allan.

Allan wakes up. He moans and looks around. His body is sore and his head throbs, but he still smiles.

Rubic wakes also. "Hey kid," he says. "I'm here." Rubic has an IV in his arm and other wires connected to him monitoring his vitals. He gets off the bed and pulls his tall metal pole decorated with fluid bags along with him to Allan's bedside. "You feeling better?"

"I feel tired," Allan says then thinks. "But I'm good."

"So we just needed to go fishing to get you talking, huh?" Rubic laughs.

"Yeah, it was definitely the fishing," Allan says sarcastically.

The nurse brings in two food trays filled with fish sticks, mashed potatoes, corn, and Jell-O. They race to see who can slurp down the Jell-O first. Allan wins.

"So why did the dam blow up?" Allan asks.

"Don't you know what was in there?" Rubic waits for an answer, but Allan's face is blank and waiting. "You don't do you?"

Allan shrugs. "I was never in there."

Rubic takes a deep breath. "It was an illegal laboratory. Some crazy lady named Alice ran it. She got away, unfortunately, but not before she triggered the explosives that she rigged all around the dam. She almost killed me, you and all those animals."

"What was the lab for?"

"She was testing on those animals. But most of the lab was destroyed, so no one knows exactly what was going on. She's a loon, for sure, a real wacko. The whole canyon and river is a crime scene now. She'd poured some crazy waste into the lake. Must have been doing it for years. We're being treated for exposure and heavy metal poisoning." Rubic ruffles Allan's hair. "I'm so proud of you for escaping. The police will want to interview you. You're gonna have to try and remember something, anything that will help them."

Allan shakes his head. "I really wasn't in there."

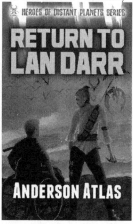

"But you came from the pipe, right? You escaped right before I got there?"

Allan's eyes narrow as he accesses his memory. "Yeah, I did come through the pipe, but I was never inside the dam." In his mind, he was never in the dam. He'd gone to a faraway place and came back through a wormhole created by the pollen.

Tears come to Allan's eyes. "I . . . saw Jibbawk. I fought it. It looked just like you said."

"That was a scary story, kiddo. I'd heard something about Jibbawk years ago. It wasn't real."

"Yes, it was," Allan mumbles.

Rubic looks away then shrugs. He isn't going to argue with Allan. Who knows what the kid had been

through or how much poison he had been exposed to. Rubic rummages through his personal belongings on the bedside table and picks out the 50's pin-up girl. He hands it to Allan. "I think you dropped this."

Allan's face scrunches. It should have been in his pocket. "Thanks, I think."

"Don't worry about any of it. We're safe now."

Later that morning Allan finds himself at the hospital window looking at the people below. He watches a jogger cut through the parking lot. Rubic gets off his bed and joins Allan at the window. He puts his arm around Allan's shoulder.

"So, you lookin' at that jogger?" Rubic asks knowing the answer to his question.

"Yeah."

"Does it still bother you? Are you hoping his legs break, and he falls on his face?"

Allan shakes his head. "Nah, I was just thinking that I never liked running anyway. Not with my legs." He did like Mizzi's mechanical legs. "And even though I can't race, I can still swim."

Rubic hugs Allan's head. "You really are gonna be okay, aren't you?"

"Yeah, I think I am."

Rubic goes back to his bed, and the doctor comes in. They talk quietly, probably about Allan, but he doesn't care. He is just happy to be safe and eating real food and in his wheelchair again.

In time, Allan gazes wearily into the cloudless blue sky and wonders about Lan Darr. Was any of it real? Did he swim in Dantia's canals? Or ride the shoulder of Lithic Fury Bink? Did he banish Jibbawk to some world ten thousand light years away? Or was it all in his mind? Was it the effect of a million poisons coursing through his body?

Asantia made a promise. When Allan turns eighteen, will he hear a knock on his window some night, open it up to the chilly air only to see Asantia sitting on the ledge holding handles connected to a cable tethered to a new, shiny airship? Will she take him off to one of a hundred crazy worlds where he'll explore the outer reaches of the galaxy? Where he'll be able to explore and see things, others only dream of? Maybe, she'll take him to visit his friend Mizzi and the Lithic Fury Bink and Lyllia of Meduna.

Allan thinks he can survive being stuck in a wheelchair, algebra, science projects, cranky teachers, two-faced people and any problem thrown at him long enough to find out. No, he *knows* he can.

The End.

DID YOU LIKE THE STORY?

Go to Amazon.com search for Strange Lands and leave me a review!

Two minutes of your time, supports this author for a LIFETIME!

Plus, the story continues.
Turn the page to find out how.

The story continues in Book 2 :

Return to Lan Darr

Go to AndersonAtlas.com/ReturnToLanDarr or to Amazon.com

Book 3: **IMMORTAL SHADOW**

go to AndersonAtlas.com/ImmortalShadow

About the Author

Anderson Atlas is an author and illustrator that lives in the hot Sonoran Desert among scaled survivors, steely eye hawks and majestic saguaros. He's an avid observer, reader and story teller. If you like his stories, help him out and leave a review or simply stay in touch by signing up for his readers group at AndersonAtlas. com

Strange Lands

Copyright 2015 Anderson Atlas

andersonatlas.com

Published by Synesthesia Books

synesthesiabooks.com

68021505R00142

Made in the USA
Charleston, SC
03 March 2017